*Suddenly, a huge sedan
barreled toward her . . .*

As she approached the car, something caught her peripheral vision. She turned as the taillights of Kim's car flashed to indicate that she'd unlocked the car. Suddenly, a huge sedan barreled toward her from the street she'd just crossed. She jumped back against the trunk of Kim's car, nearly pinned by the approaching vehicle. When it was only inches from her it stopped. Headlights came on and blinded her. She squinted, and threw her arm across her eyes, frozen in the beam like a deer on a country road.

HEAR NO EVIL

Death in the Afternoon
Missing!
A Time of Fear

HEAR NO EVIL

Missing!

Kate Chester

SCHOLASTIC INC.
New York Toronto London Auckland Sydney

ISBN 0-590-67327-0

12 11 10 9 8 7 6 5 4 3 2   6 7 8 9/9 0 1/0

Printed in the U.S.A.   01

First Scholastic printing, August 1996

To the Reader:

Sara Howell is profoundly, postlingually deaf (meaning she lost her hearing after she learned to speak). She is fluent in American Sign Language (ASL), and English. She can read lips.

When a character speaks, quotation marks are used: "Watch out for that bus!" When a character signs, *italics* are used to indicate ASL: *Watch out for that bus!* Quotation marks and *italics* indicate the character is signing and speaking simultaneously: *"Watch out for that bus!"*

Unless the sign is described (for example: Sara circled her heart. *I'm sorry . . .*), the italicized words are translations of ASL into English, not literal descriptions of the grammatical structure of American Sign Language.

HEAR NO EVIL

Missing!

Chapter 1

The minute Sara Howell saw the cola commercial, she grabbed her brother and urged him to the television set. *K-I-M-B-E-R-L-Y R-O-T-H.* She didn't have a name sign for Kim which forced her to finger spell each letter. *The model in the magazine picture tacked on my bulletin board.* She waited for Steve to decipher the manual symbols. He nodded wearily and looked at the screen.

In the commercial, Kim Roth, Sara's glamorous Radley Academy classmate, drove her fire-engine-red sports car along a deserted road lined with cornfields. Her blonde hair blew away from her face. Suddenly she stopped the car and jumped out. Her faded jeans stopped at mid-thigh. She winked at a perfect boy changing a flat tire. Then she popped open a can of soda, sipped from it, and offered it to the gorgeous boy. EXPECT THE UNEXPECTED flashed on the screen.

Steve signed with raised eyebrows. *She's only sixteen?*

Sara signed back. *Same as me.*

Her brother frowned. *Actress, model. Fast life. Fast friends.* He'd just come home after a grueling shift at the detective bureau of the Radley Police Department's Fourth Precinct. He needed dinner first; a look at the mail; some television or the newspaper. Sara knew better than to hit him with anything the least bit controversial. Kimberly Roth and her spur-of-the-moment sleepover invitation was just that.

Be patient. Don't push, Sara told herself as Steve dropped into the easy chair and stretched his jean-clad legs out in front of him. He worked his feet out of his boots and wiggled a toe through the hole in his sock. As a plainclothes detective he dressed like he was still a criminal justice major at Radley University. He was young enough to pass for one.

That was the problem. At twenty-two Stephen Howell was Sara's legal guardian, but their grandparents or the state's Department of Social Services could change that the minute they decided the rookie detective was too busy, too young, too inexperienced . . . too anything to take on responsibility for his sixteen-year-old orphaned sister. Steve closed his eyes.

Sara had lost her hearing as the result of an illness at the end of kindergarten. Although the whole family had studied American Sign Language, Sara had left their home in Radley at the end of elementary school, when her mother died, to board at the Edgewood School for the Deaf. Living away from home meant that during her entire adolescence, she hadn't spent more than vacations with her brother. In August the sudden hit-and-run death of their father, a senior detective in Radley's police force, changed everything.

In the two months since, her life had turned upside down, home had changed from the cocoon of the deaf community at Edgewood to the Howells' Thurston Court city apartment in Radley. Sara was back in a hearing school, in a hearing environment, with a hearing brother. They only had each other, and it was harder than Sara had imagined. Steve had trouble understanding her muffled speech; she couldn't always read his lips. His awkward signing often made him hard to understand.

She tapped his shoulder and spoke as she signed. *"Sleepover tonight. No boys. No wild party. Keesha's going, too. Talk to Keesha's mom. Mrs. Fletcher will make you feel better."*

"I can't run across the hall to Brenda Fletcher every time there's a problem."

Sara nodded. *"Yes you can. She wants to help. She got me into her school, got me an interpreter. . . . She's always helped."*

"I save the Fletchers for the big stuff." *Big stuff.* Steve tried to reply with his hands which only added to his frustration as he fumbled the signs.

Say again, Sara tried.

Don't know K-I-M. Don't know her. Don't know her parents, he reiterated. He wiggled his fingers as if his joints hurt, then gave up. *Don't know this girl.*

Sara wanted to tell him to stop feeling pressured to be the perfect father figure, and let her go to Kim's. Instead she ruffled the fur of Tuck, her hearing-ear golden retriever, and stared at the television set. Her overly protective, watchful, sheltering, guardian of a big brother would make up his mind when he was good and ready.

Two hours later Sara and her best friend Keesha Fletcher finished their pizza in the Roths' designer kitchen. The housekeeper said goodnight to Kim. Sara nudged Keesha. *I didn't know her parents were away. DO NOT TELL STEVE. WORRY. WORRY. WORRY.*

Keesha laughed. *Kim's mother is away on business. Kansas City. Her dad does investments or something. Has to travel, too. Both back tomorrow afternoon.*

"I'm so glad you guys could come over," Kim said as she returned from the door. "Tonight is usually aerobics class, but my teacher canceled the session. This will be a lot more fun than working myself into a sweat."

Sara frowned in apology as she lost the last part of the sentence.

More fun than sweaty exercise, Keesha translated.

Kim tapped Sara's arm. "Signing is so cool. I could hardly take my eyes off you and your interpreter that first day you were in my English class. You've got to teach me." She leaned over to pet her miniature poodle.

Sara snapped her fingers and puckered as if she were whistling: the sign for dog.

Kim repeated it, then grinned. *Dog.*

Sara moved one hand over the other: *Tonight.* Then she spoke as she signed. *"You need a name sign. Something that means K-I-M, so you don't have to finger spell every time. Start with the first letter of your name. Then add something that's part of you, or important to you . . . whatever. Tonight we'll think of one."* She signed the letter *K.*

"So glad your brother said you could stay over," Keesha added to Sara as Kim practiced her letter.

Sara wrapped her first three fingers over

her thumb to sign *M*. She pushed her fist forward twice as Keesha laughed. *M. M*. It stood for *minor miracle,* their shorthand for anything controversial that Steve agreed to. She repeated it and *DOG* as Kim's first lesson.

The miracle had been a phone call. In the middle of arguing about Kim's invitation, Steve had been called on a case. Sara had convinced him that she would be better off at Kimberly Roth's than home by herself. It was the truth. After all she and her brother had been through in solving the death of their father, she much preferred company to the dark rooms and silent corridors of their apartment when Steve was working.

The Roths' townhouse was as spectacular as Keesha had said. Winchester Commons hugged a ridge above the Buckeye River. Even in the dark there were million-dollar views of the water and Radley's cityscape. Kim's room had French doors to its own balcony.

The artwork was real and the cut flowers were fresh. Family members smiled from dozens of silver frames. In each snapshot, if they weren't holding skis or raising sails, they were in front of the Eiffel Tower, a pyramid, an Alp, or Lenin's Tomb.

"Two half brothers, and three half sisters from my parents' first marriages," Kim said.

Sara admired the shots and showed her the ASL signs for brother and sister.

"They're all much older, on their own. You won't find me in these pictures much. I was always home with the nanny, or the housekeeper, or whoever Mom or Dad could find to put up with me. I think I could disappear and they wouldn't know I was missing for a week." Kim led the group into the study. She swept her arm toward the walls. "Never mind. This is *my* gallery."

From little girls' dresses, to designer jeans, to a blowup from the latest cola commercial, ten years of Kimberly Roth's modeling life hung in simple Plexiglas frames. There were even Playbills from road companies of Broadway shows in which Kim had played small roles.

Sara and Kim were the same height and shared a slim, athletic build, and hair that hung below their shoulders, but the similarity stopped there. Kim had lightened her hair to a glistening blonde. Sara's was a warm brown.

Sara studied the photographs and smiled ruefully. "I'll teach you to sign if you teach me to be glamorous."

Kim laughed. "Anybody looks good with ten pounds of makeup, designer clothes, and six photographer's assistants running after you with blow-dryers and mascara." She pointed to a shot of herself in a short, jade-green dress. "To make that fit, they put clothespins all the way up the back."

Sara tapped Kim's shoulder. "Name sign. I have the perfect name sign for you." She separated her index and middle fingers to sign *K*, then formed a rectangle at her face: CAMERA. K, CAMERA. "It means Kim."

"Thank you! It's perfect! Right now the camera, and keeping in shape for it, are about my whole life." She tapped her chest. "Let me do all our names, the way you two do them." She made a *K* and hooked her index fingers: *K, friend: Keesha.* "Sara," she added and formed *S, friend.*

Perfect, Sara signed.

"Did you make them up?" Kim asked.

Keesha nodded. "In kindergarten. After Sara got sick and lost her hearing, our parents thought it would help if I took ASL lessons with her, so I could learn her new language."

"It's a beautiful language. It's so pretty to watch. Let's go hit a coffee bar, maybe pick up a video, and you can give me lessons." Kim pantomimed turning a steering wheel.

Sara laughed and held up her index finger to get her to watch and guess what she was saying. *I love your car.*

"*Love.* I got that one. *Car?* You love my car?"

The sleek black import with the KIMZ vanity license plate was the envy of the class. "Gorgeous car," Sara replied. Her mouth dropped open as Kim threw her the keys.

"Go to it! It's around the corner in the parking area next to the common. The garage is filled with my parents' cars." She pointed at the dark window. "My car's in bay number seven." She held up seven fingers. "Keesha and I'll clean up the pizza, lock up, and meet you out front. You can drive us through the complex, till we get out to Riverside Drive and traffic."

Sara pointed her finger at Kim and swept her hand to the right. *Go to it?* she signed.

Go to it. Kim repeated it with a laugh.

Sara grabbed her purse and jacket and hurried down the brick walk. After the comfortable, secure environment of the Edgewood School for the Deaf, adjusting to a hearing world and hearing friends took as much work as accepting the fact that she was an orphan and Steve was her guardian.

Steve constantly reminded her that every day would get a little easier, and it was Keesha who insisted that friends would come, once her classmates got to know her. Maybe they were right. Kimberly Roth thought the ability to sign was as exotic as she thought modeling was. She couldn't help but feel that there was a friendship in the making.

She watched her shadow move as she passed in and out of the glow from gaslights that lined the curb. The hilly terrain above the river was lined with handsome townhouses. The parking bay for overflow cars was around the corner, between the Roths' complex and the next cluster of buildings. Although there was no traffic, a sixth sense made her stop and look over her shoulder. She was suddenly nervous.

The October night smelled of fall. The air was crisp. There'd be frost soon. She rubbed her arms against the chill. When she was sure there was nothing disturbing the night, she crossed the street.

Sara watched the stars dance over the river while she approached the cars parked side by side under a carport shelter. KIMZ was right where it was supposed to be. Number seven.

As she approached the car, something caught her peripheral vision. She turned as the taillights of Kim's car flashed to indicate that she'd unlocked the car. Suddenly, a huge sedan barreled toward her from the street she'd just crossed. She jumped back against the trunk of Kim's car, nearly pinned by the approaching vehicle. When it was only inches from her it stopped. Headlights came on and blinded her. She squinted, and threw her arm across her eyes, frozen in the beam like a deer on a country road.

Chapter 2

As quickly as the headlights came on, they went back off. The car backed up and made a screeching U-turn. Sara caught a glimpse of a blonde woman in the passenger seat — as scared as she — who turned to yell at the driver as he tore down the street. The red blur of brake lights broke the darkness as the sedan careened around the corner out of sight.

Sara's heart hammered and pounded as fear kept her pressed against Kim's car. The metal dug into the backs of her legs. She tried to catch her breath as she unconsciously tapped her ear. *She hadn't heard the car!* She *couldn't* have heard the car! And without headlights . . .

Her hands shook as she got into Kim's car and put the key in the ignition. Her deafness usually made her more alert, more attentive. She tapped her forehead. *Stupid.* She could have been killed. Kim's car could have been smashed. Slowly, after half a dozen deep breaths, she backed onto the street. She gripped the steering wheel and drove at a snail's pace around the bend to the townhouses.

Kim and Keesha were locking the front door, and waved as Sara pulled up to the curb. She slid across into the passenger seat and opened the door so the interior light would illuminate the three of them.

"You can drive us out to the entrance — Sara?" Kim stopped in midsentence.

Sara shook her head. "No more driving." She tapped her ear. "Did you hear anything? Brakes? A screech of tires?"

Both girls shook their heads.

"A car came flying at me, out of nowhere. No lights until I was nearly pinned against your bumper. Whoever was driving . . . racing! Huge hurry." Sara tapped her ears again. "Couldn't hear anything; never saw it."

Kim's eyes widened in sympathy. "I'm so sorry. Kids come out here to hang out in the common because it's not patrolled as much as the town parks. Cars get stolen. You probably saved mine."

Sara tried to smile.

"There are guards," Kim continued, "but they have a lot of ground to cover. Could you identify anybody?"

Sara shrugged. "Not the car. A woman in the passenger seat. Blonde. I hardly saw her. Scared as I was! Car was dark. Big." She shrugged an apology.

Kim shuddered and peered through her windshield. She glanced slowly back to her friends. "I'm sure glad you guys are spending the night."

She closed the door and put the car into drive. They were silent until they'd left the entrance to the complex and were out on fashionable Riverside Drive. Traffic was normal; there was no sign of the big car Sara had described. If someone had been bent on stealing Kim's car, Sara had come along at the right time.

When Sara was calmer, she didn't want to talk about the car. She changed the subject to Kim's latest TV commercial. "We should be passing cornfields, spotting gorgeous boys changing tires, drinking cola," Sara said. Kim frowned and looked embarrassed that she didn't understand Sara's speech. Sara turned to the backseat and signed for Keesha to interpret her muffled voice.

Keesha's dark features were still serious, but she leaned forward and repeated what Sara had said in her own, clear voice. Kim nodded, then laughed.

Sara brought her closed hand down from her lips. *Thank you.* She and Keesha had been best friends since the Fletchers moved across the hall when both girls were five. The fact that the Fletchers were black never put any strain on their friendship. Keesha had been through everything with her: the loss of her hearing, the loss of her mother, and the recent loss of her father. Before deafness, before Edgewood, there had been Keesha. Now, as Sara struggled with hearing friends and the pressures of being mainstreamed into a hearing school, there was still Keesha to help.

Kim maneuvered the car from Riverside Drive through the residential neighborhoods. She saluted as they passed the Radley Academy campus where they were all in the Upper School, and then turned north toward the university area. Traffic increased until the avenues were busy. The city streets were lined with bookstores, record shops, and funky clothing lofts that catered to college students. They drove to a coffeehouse they all liked.

I can't believe it, a free table outside! Sara signed to the girls as she hurried to grab it. Parking had taken twice the normal time in order to find a place secure enough for Kim to leave her car. They settled on a curbside space near the corner, directly beneath a streetlight. It made Sara appreciate her father's green sedan. There was little worry that anyone would steal it.

High school and college students gathered at the alley entrance that gave the Side Door

Café its name. The coveted table was one of ten that filled the sidewalk in front of the café. They were under an emerald-and-white awning that flapped in the breeze. From the earliest sign of spring until the tables were taken in after the first hard freeze in the fall, the patio was packed. Despite the October chill, the girls took the one vacant table and ordered dessert and coffee. "Chocolate," Sara sniffed as they waited for their order.

Keesha sniffed the air, too, and nodded. "The breeze must be easterly. Delicious!"

Although the café was blocks from the Buckeye Foods bakery, the cookie factory often filled Radley's air with the delicious scent of chocolate, vanilla, and spices. It made the Side Door Café all the more popular.

When their orders arrived, Kim sipped her cinnamon-flavored coffee, still craning her neck to try and keep an eye on her car.

"Relax," Sara said and showed her the sign.

"Sorry. I love that car!" Kim turned to face Sara, so she could read her lips clearly. "Anyway, this is a great place on Sunday nights.

Lots of kids. Poets even get up and read their work."

Keesha put down her mug. "Who do you come here with on Sundays for the poetry? I could never get away. Sunday night's family dinner and homework time at our place. That's what happens when your mother's a school principal . . . in your own school."

Kim looked thoughtful. Her blue eyes were dark. "That's why I started coming. Sunday nights at our place mean one of my parents is packing to leave Monday morning, or just arriving home and exhausted after a hard week of vacation or making money."

Keesha smiled. *"Sara, you should come here with Bret."* Instead of finger spelling Sara's boyfriend's name, she used his name sign: the letter *B* and the symbol for *VOICE:* open index and middle finger across her neck.

When Kim looked confused, Sara added, *"B, VOICE is B-R-E-T. His parents are deaf. They gave him that name sign when he was born hearing and could speak for them when they needed it."*

Kim practiced the signs: first Bret's, then

hers, Keesha's, and Sara's. She moved from names to other nouns and by the time they had finished their drinks, Kim had signed everything from her review of *DOG*, to *STREET, STORE, COOKIE*, and other words. The only thing that slowed her down was her constant glancing up the street.

"Don't worry," Keesha said more than once.

Sara nodded. *"It's not like that guy in the car tonight followed us. It's done. Over. Relax."* But inwardly Sara was still frightened.

Sorry. Kim proudly circled her heart as Sara had taught her.

"If you'll feel better, we can stop at the police station and tell my brother."

"I think we should," Kim replied.

When they'd finished their coffees, Keesha said, "Let's rent a mystery video after we talk to Steve, something with a lot of action."

Sara frowned. *"Action! Almost getting run over was enough action for me."* She shivered slightly.

Keesha suddenly looked up into the awning and said to Kim, "That's the second time I've heard that groaning noise. Do you hear it?"

Frustration at being left out of the conversation made Sara turn away, but as she did, motion caught her eye. It wasn't sound, but sight that brought her to her feet. Directly over them the green awning dropped to a dangerous angle. Fabric split. A wedge of night sky suddenly appeared and Sara grabbed Kim's arm. Keesha's brown eyes widened in fear as the awning jerked precariously. The entire frame had pulled loose from the building. As the awning ripped from the brick siding, Keesha put her arm up to shield her face. The awning crashed onto the patio. It covered everyone who had been sitting there with a suffocating blackness. Underneath it, tables, chairs, and people tumbled together. Screams filled the air.

Chapter 3

Sara lay where she had fallen and pressed her open hand against the damp stain soaking the leg of her jeans. In the dark, unrelenting silence she could feel the panicked scramble of people trying to free themselves. Someone knocked into her and she was pushed back against a fallen chair. When light finally sliced the blackness, she realized that people were frantically cutting away the heavy canvas from its bent frame.

Light from the streetlamps cast weird shadows. Keesha lay on her side, pressing her hand against her head. Kim lay dazed under the weight of a table. Sara got up and helped a waiter yank at the torn canvas until it was wide enough to step through. The two of them eased Keesha to the curb and sat her down. "It's my arm," Keesha said as she held her left arm gingerly.

Don't move, Keesha. I'm sure help is on the way. Sara looked back at Kim who was pushing away a woman who had her gripped by the elbow and was easing her to her feet. Sara stumbled over chairs and broken dishes and glasses until she reached them. "Are you okay?"

Kim shook her head. Her hand was in her hair. "No, but I can get myself to the hospital," she said to the woman.

Sara and the woman exchanged glances. The woman finally let go of Kim and turned to others, still under the fallen canvas. A few students lay motionless, but most, like Sara, had cuts and abrasions. Sara helped Kim over to Keesha, who was still at the curb.

Pandemonium struck as waiters, then passersby, ran to the chaotic scene. The night was a blur of victims and those scrambling to free them. Traffic snarled on the street. Students righted chairs, offered ice and napkins to those who were bleeding. Another group kept curious onlookers back.

By the time the street was flashing with the familiar blue and red whirl of police lights and ambulances, Sara had stopped the flow of blood through her jeans with a pack of napkins someone had handed her. She had no idea how deep the wound was in her calf. Dark stains soaked her pant leg. "I hope it looks worse than it is," she said to Kim.

Kim brushed her blonde hair from her eyes, but her fingers came back sticky with blood. "My head won't stop bleeding. At least my face wasn't cut."

Keesha put her good arm around Kim. "Help's coming."

"I've already had too much help." She looked back at the chaos. "That woman kept insisting that she could drive me to the hospital. I kept telling her there were three of us. She said she only had room for one." She winced and looked from Keesha to Sara. "I wasn't about to leave you guys."

Sara turned to Kim and said slowly, "You know, she looked like the woman who was the passenger in the car that almost ran me over. Do you know her?"

Kim shook her head. "I've never seen her before."

Sara signed, *Probably just imagining things.*

The emergency entrance of East End General Hospital was crowded. Four ambulances had transported anyone bleeding or hit by the falling awning. The majority of the patrons had escaped serious injury, but two had arrived in neck braces and on backboards. Inside, the emergency room was a blur of activity. Nurses ran; orderlies arrived with gurneys. Patients already there, waiting for their problems to be taken care of, watched helplessly as they were temporarily forgotten. The bank of pay phones along one wall was crowded with people talking or waiting to call their families. Kim managed to grab a receiver and punch in the Fletchers' number for Keesha.

By the time the admitting secretary reached Kim, Keesha, and Sara for their medical information, the Fletchers had arrived. Keesha's mother hovered over the three of them while her husband John supplied insurance information and authorized treatment for his daughter.

"I called Steve," Brenda Fletcher said. "But the station told me he was already on his way. He answered the call as a general emergency. Sara, he doesn't know you're here. Stay put till he arrives. Do you need an interpreter?"

She shook her head.

"Then I'll go with Keesha." She hugged Sara and followed as Keesha, still cradling her arm, was whisked into the examining area.

Sara stared at the phones and tried not to look around the all-too-familiar surroundings. She had been here Black Saturday. It was her term for the August night she and Steve had been called to meet the ambulance that delivered senior detective Paul Howell to the entrance twenty feet from where she sat. Stay put, Brenda Fletcher had said. Sara wanted to be anywhere but where she was. She refused to look at the sliding doors. Her father had been in an accident, too, one that turned out to be murder.

She felt light-headed. Sweat broke out on her face. She didn't want to think about this place and the awful memories it held. Kim was asking something but she couldn't understand. She leaned over and put her head between her knees, but as she toppled forward she fell against someone who lifted her up.

"Steve!" she mumbled as her brother engulfed her in a tight hug. *Keesha's mom called the station,* she managed as she looked into his shocked face.

He frowned. "What are you doing here? The accident's on every scanner on both sides of the river. You were at the Side Door Café? You told me you would be at your friend's at Winchester Commons."

We went to get a coffee and video. We were coming to see you. Kim's car was nearly stolen. Steve, this place — I started to faint. Get me out of here. I can't stay. She half stood, only to have him gently push her back into her seat.

Let go, Sara. Don't let the memories rule you. Understand? "You're not alone in this. It hits me every time I come over here."

She looked at him hard, to make sure she'd understood. *You, too?*

Sure. Me, too. As he fumbled with the signs, he spoke. "I promise I'll get you out of here as soon as a doctor looks you over. Hang on till then. I know you can. We've been through worse."

She managed a weak smile.

Hurt? He pushed his index fingers toward each other. *Do you need an interpreter?*

Not too bad. Sara showed him her leg. She was interrupted by the return of the administrator, a young woman who recognized her brother.

"Detective Howell, isn't it?"

He stood up. "Steve Howell. Turns out my sister was one of the casualties. Sara — my sister," he added by way of an introduction. "Sara, this is Marisa Douglas."

"Sara Howell," the administrator repeated. "I should have made the connection. Steve, it's a good thing you're here. We need you to authorize medical care. The whole awning pulled off the front of the Side Door Café."

He nodded. "I drove past it." He forked his

index and middle fingers at his eyes. *Saw it. Terrible.* As if just realizing they weren't alone, he glanced at Kim who'd been given a gauze pad to press on the cut on her arm and one for her scalp wound. He circled his heart. "*Sorry.* You must be Kim Roth. I'm Steve Howell, Sara's brother. Has anyone looked at you yet? How's your head?"

Kim blushed as she looked up into his concerned expression. "They said it was superficial and to press this on the cut until somebody can see me."

"Are your folks on the way?"

Kim shook her head. "They're both out of town. One's in Chicago, the other's in Kansas City."

"Not home?" He shot another studied look at Sara.

She signed an apology. *I didn't know her parents wouldn't be home, I swear. It wouldn't have mattered. We just went out to rent a video and have coffee.*

Marisa turned to Kim. "Have you called your parents? One of them will have to authorize treatment."

Kim shook her head. "Not yet. The phones

are tied up. I haven't thought of much except my head — and Sara."

"She'll be all right," Steve said. "This place has a lot of ugly memories for both of us. Let me call for you. Do you have a phone number where they can be reached?"

"My father's at the Kansas City Royale. I left the number at home. I'm okay, really. Nothing hurts very much. The nurse said the bleeding will stop."

"Let Steve call for you," Marisa added. "You need to be checked and the doctors will need authorization."

Before she could protest, Steve put his hand on her arm. "I'll see what I can do. Sit tight." He looked back at his sister. "We'll get you out of here, but you're both coming back to our place. Where's Keesha?"

"The Fletchers are with her. I think they took her to get x-rayed."

Kim sat up. "We'll be fine back at my house, really, Steve," she replied, still looking up into his blue eyes.

"Not tonight." He continued to brush off her protests and after speaking into his police portable, moved with Marisa to the pay phones.

Kim looked at Sara. "Whoa. Talk about feeling faint. He's really good-looking."

Sara grimaced. "Good-looking or not, now he'll worry that every time I go out, buildings are going to fall on me."

Chapter 4

The group returned to Thurston Court in a caravan that included the Fletchers' station wagon, Kim's import driven by a police officer, and Steve's unmarked police car. The Fletchers parked in the tenants' garage, while Kim's car was parked in one of the guest slots that flanked the brick courtyard at the entrance to the building.

X rays had revealed that Keesha's arm wasn't broken, but it was bruised seriously enough that she went home medicated, with an ice pack and a sling to keep the arm immobile. Sara and Kim had lacerations that required cleaning and bandages, but no sutures.

"Do you know how lucky you were?" Steve asked as he put the guest pass on Kim's windshield. "At least three people were hospitalized." He frowned and moved his index fingers toward each other. *Hurt.*

I know. I'm okay. Tired, Sara signed.

"At the hospital you said you were coming to see me. Somebody tried to steal Kim's car?"

"Wild night," Sara replied and immediately regretted it. Her brother didn't need anything else to alarm him.

Steve arched his eyebrows. "I'm coming upstairs long enough for you two to tell me what happened."

"Not much to tell. K-I-M can explain," Sara said as they entered the apartment. She stopped to greet her retriever Tuck, then nudged her friend. Kim gave the rookie detective all the details Sara had given her hours earlier.

"Do you want to file a report?"

Kim shook her head. "We're not even sure the car was being stolen. Sara thinks a woman who tried to help me at the café might have been in the passenger seat of the car that almost ran her over. It could have been some couple out joyriding who just didn't see Sara. Since she can't hear, maybe she didn't know they were coming, and didn't know to get out of the way as they tore by."

"With their headlights off?"

"Who knows. Anyway, my car's safe and sound downstairs, and we're safe and sound up here. That's all I care about."

Steve sighed. "As soon as I get you two settled, I have to get back to the station. There's already a rumor that someone was seen fooling with the awning's bolts at the café. Kim, call your father and tell him everything's all right. He wanted a full report after he gave his consent for the medical attention. He'll be glad it wasn't anything serious."

"He'll be glad it didn't interfere with his schedule," she replied.

Steve glanced at Sara. She shrugged.

"Sara's teaching me ASL," Kim said abruptly. She looked at Tuck and signed *dog*. "I have a name sign already." She signed *K, Camera*. Steve smiled and repeated it and Kim blushed. "Show me yours."

Steve signed *S* and slid his thumb and

index finger from forehead to wrist. *Brother.*
"Sara thought it up when she was six, before
she got creative."

Sara smiled. "Here's his real name." She
frowned, then added her wrists and forearms
in two quick gestures.

"What! Tell me what she signed."

"*S, Strong-Guard-Cop,*" he said as he repeated the signs. "I think she means jailer."

Kim repeated it, but Steve pushed her
hands down. "No thanks. *S, Brother* will do
just fine."

They all laughed and Kim signed, *Thank
you.* "Thanks for letting me stay here. After
all that's happened, I don't know — you
were right, I guess I do feel better over here."

"The Fletchers are right across the hall. I
want Sara where I can reach her on the TTY,
if I have to." He nodded toward the tele-
communication machine that augmented the
phone by printing out the conversation.

"Any relay operator on any phone would
be enough," Sara protested.

Steve pointed at her. "Never mind. Just
stay here and rest. I walked Tuck before I
left. He's all set for the night. Get a good

night's sleep. I'll be back some time after two. With all this mess at the café, it'll be a long night."

"Will the police investigate?" Kim asked.

"Sure, especially if the injuries turn out to be life threatening, and these rumors keep flying. There are building codes to prevent this kind of thing. There's a lot ahead of me tonight. Don't wake me up when you get up in the morning." He grinned. "Kim, you keep Sara from slamming every cabinet in the kitchen. She has no idea how loud she is when I'm still trying to sleep."

Fifteen minutes later the apartment was quiet. Kim had borrowed a nightshirt and called her father.

"Everything all right?" Sara asked as they settled into her twin beds.

"Couldn't be better. I didn't cost them any money or foul up their plans for the evening. Actually my mother was already asleep. Dad sounded pretty tired, too."

"They work hard." *Hard work.* As Kim begrudgingly nodded, Sara pointed to Tuck, curled up at the doorway. "In the morning I have to take him for his walk. You sleep in. When you get up, I'll loan you something to wear and we'll go see how Keesha's doing."

"Let's make her brunch and surprise her. I'll make sure we don't make noise and wake up Steve."

"Good idea. Sorry about my brother. He's way too protective." Sara sighed. "I wish I had your freedom."

"Freedom? My parents don't have time to care. Mom does her stuff to prove to Dad she didn't marry him for his money. Dad has to run around making sure his millions keep making millions. I have my own life so I don't complicate theirs. Don't ever be sorry about Steve." *Steve*. She signed it properly again. "He's gorgeous; he cares about you; he's practically a Radley hero. You are so lucky and I'm so jealous."

Sara thought she had misread Kim's lips. She flipped her fist with outstretched pinky finger away from her mouth. *"Jealous?"*

Kim repeated it. "Does he date anybody special?"

"Special? He dates, but he says there's no time for special; no time for love. Don't get any ideas about Steve. He's too old for you, twenty-two!" She flashed her fingers for emphasis.

"I've dated guys that old," Kim said.

Sara shook her head, suddenly glad they never made it as far as the police station, the way they'd planned. If Kimberly Roth had seen Steve Howell decked out like a detective in the Interrogation Room with his revolver strapped on and the wanted posters on the bulletin board, she'd probably run away just so he could rescue her.

There had to be a diplomatic way to tell her that Steve had no interest in his younger sister's little high school friends.

When they had turned off the bedroom lights, Sara stared up at the dark ceiling. She tried to concentrate on Kim and her crush, but even under two wool blankets she was cold. She could see the shadowy car racing toward her. She could feel the suffocating darkness under the café's awning. Tears slipped down her cheeks. The silence in the room was awful.

Chapter 5

The next morning the October sun barely topped the roofs as Sara signed hello to John O'Connor, the Thurston Court doorman. She led Tuck through the lobby and out the court-yard entrance of the building. Her leg was stiff, and the bandage pulled as she limped.

She took Tuck to the walkway that bordered the visitors' parking area. Kim's car was safely placed between two others. KIMZ. Sara looked at the license plate and admired the car. For a girl who had everything, Kim wasn't very happy. She had more affection for her car than her parents. Sara thought about telling her how lucky she was just to have parents, even if they were distracted by their own lives.

Sara was still in her first semester at Radley Academy, but she knew that many of her classmates considered Kim a snob. It was true that Kim could be standoffish, and she was certainly glamorous, but Sara wondered how those classmates would react if they knew she went to poetry readings alone, and spent Friday nights downtown at aerobics classes.

Sara crossed the street with Tuck and paid little attention to the cars until a dark sedan drew up to the light. The driver stared at her. Her heart jumped involuntarily. She stared back, but the driver looked at something on the dashboard.

She broke into a limping trot with Tuck, but her shin began to throb where the awning had hit it. As she turned around, the car entered the Thurston Court courtyard and circled the visitors' parking spaces. There were available spaces, but the doorman was a stickler for rules. If this driver tried to park, John O'Connor would be out in a flash to tell him he needed a pass from a tenant, proof that he was supposed to be there.

Just as she'd guessed, John O'Connor was

halfway down the walkway by the time limped toward him. However, instead of a polite exchange, the car leapt forward and sped across the pavement. Like the night before, Sara — and the doorman — had to jump back to get out of the way. Before she could get a second look at the driver, the car was on the street and gone from view.

John O'Connor grabbed Sara. "Are you all right?"

Sara tried to breathe slowly. "I think so." But she knew she wasn't.

"Twice in twenty-four hours?" Kim asked as Sara relayed the story when she returned to the apartment. Kim was already in the kitchen pulling brunch together. "Could it be the same sedan? What if they had followed me and found the car?"

Sara had to put her hand on Kim's arm to keep her from running for the door. "Your car — and you — are fine here. Both cars in a hurry, that's for sure, but the same? Too much of a coincidence. Besides, I think there's a good chance the driver last night just didn't see me. Just now the driver proba-

bly only wanted to get away from the doorman." Sara wanted to believe that.

"Sara, you're always in the wrong place at
the wrong time. No wonder your brother
worries."

"He's not going to worry about this because I'm not going to tell him." Sara turned
her attention to her guest. She gave Kim the
once-over and sighed in admiration. Even in
a borrowed outfit, Kim somehow managed to
make Sara's oversized bib jeans and skinny
ribbed sweater look like they belonged on the
cover of one of her fashion magazines.

Kim put silverware on the counter. "After
we eat and take some brunch to Keesha, why
don't we come back over here and fix something for Steve? He needs a thank-you for
everything he did for us last night."

Steve again. Sara took her time answering.
Kim had pinned her hair into a stylish knot
that avoided the bandage at the nape of her
neck. Her scalp must still be as sore as Sara's
leg. Sara got the distinct impression that Kim
was dressing for the rookie detective who'd
come off his shift at two A.M.

"Steve needs to sleep," Sara finally replied.

"Don't worry about him. Last night was just part of his job." She waited to make sure Kim understood and winced at the hurt expression on her friend's face. "Forget Steve. You're too young," she added when Kim turned to her. "There's more, too. He's my guardian. Has to work with Department of Social Services. His life has to be perfect. He'd lose custody of me if he dated my friends. Understand?"

Kim nodded, even though her expression was skeptical.

"Then I couldn't live here," Sara added.

"But you've told me you loved your Deaf school."

"Still do, but too far from Steve. We need each other now." She bit her lip against the ache. Kim seemed to realize that she didn't want to discuss all the changes the past few months had brought, and didn't ask any more questions. "His job gets dangerous," Sara continued. "Too dangerous for falling in love."

Kim straightened her shoulders. "Who said anything about love? I wouldn't know love if it jumped out of that car you saw this morning and bit me." She changed the subject. "Okay, let's surprise Keesha with food — brunch."

Ten minutes later they crossed the hall to the Fletchers' door with a tray of toasted bagels, herbed cream cheese, fruit, juice and a mug of tea. Keesha opened the door. She had the *Radley Gazette* tucked under her arm. The lead story read:

CAFÉ AWNING COLLAPSE INJURES DOZENS
INVESTIGATION WARRANTED
POLICE DETECTIVE'S SISTER AMONG THE
INJURED

"What are they investigating?" Kim asked.

"I guess they don't think it was an accident," Keesha said.

Sara remembered what Steve had said.

An hour later they returned to the apartment with Keesha and an empty tray. Steve was in the living room with a cup of coffee. He stood up and hugged Keesha. "Feeling better?"

"Sore, that's all. And full, thanks to Sara and Kim."

"How about some eggs, Steve?" Kim asked. "I saw some in your refrigerator." Before anyone could stop her, she disappeared into the kitchen.

News from the station about the accident? Sara asked Steve.

He shook his head. "Nothing yet. The owners insist the building's up to code . . . inspected . . . all that. There were no really serious injuries, thank goodness. You sure you girls are feeling all right?"

"We're feeling fine." Keesha yanked her thumb toward the kitchen. "I hope you're feeling hungry."

Kim had filled the counter with what looked like the entire contents of the refrigerator. Steve frowned at Sara. In reply Sara shook her head. It didn't appear that her admonitions had made any difference. Kimberly Roth was obviously used to doing what she wanted. And she seemed to want Steve.

Chapter Six

*D*oes danger follow you, or do you follow danger? Bret Sanderson signed.

Bret's gestures were short, direct stabs in the air. His handsome face was full of concern. Body language was crucial in interpreting ASL, and she didn't like what she saw.

I don't need another Steve.

No, you need some common sense, he signed back.

Common sense wouldn't have kept the awning from falling on me. Maybe I shouldn't have told you everything about Friday night. She bit her lip in frustration. It was Sunday evening, an evening they'd almost ruined by arguing.

She'd met Bret Sanderson at the city library. The tall, handsome basketball player worked after school and some weekends until the season started. She was looking forward to watching him play for Penham School, even though it was a local rival. Because Bret's parents were deaf, he was fluent in ASL and English. He sometimes interpreted for Sara and Steve when they couldn't understand each other. In a dozen ways since she'd left Edgewood, Bret made communicating in the hearing world easier. She talked to him regularly on the TTY, told him her problems, and shared her secrets. Now, as they were about to leave her apartment, he brought up everything she'd told him over the dinner she'd made for them, including the information Steve had given her Saturday night: the police and building inspector had confirmed that the awning at the Side Door Café had been tampered with.

Be realistic, Sara. The investigation uncovers creepy stuff with the awning —

Nothing to do with me!

Except you were under it! You could have been really hurt at the café, not to mention the mess with Kim's car. You're limping . . .

bruised . . . I'm not angry. I care about you, that's all.

I know and I'm glad. She circled her heart. *Just don't worry so much.*

He kissed her. A slow kiss that made her warm and happy. *I have to admit, this is more fun than fighting.* This time he did grin.

It was dusk Thursday evening by the time Radley Academy's crew team returned to school after their usual practice at the boathouse on Shelter Island. Sara, Keesha, and their friend Liz Martinson were all members. Sara's limp had improved and Keesha was out of her sling. It was the first practice for both of them since the accident. They piled out of the school van, and started for their rides home.

As Sara signed good-bye to Liz and turned back to Keesha, Kimberly Roth's car arrived in the parking lot. The window slid down effortlessly, but when neither girl responded, Kim got out of the car and flagged them down. Sara shook her head as Kim rushed to them. The more Sara got to know her, the more breathless Kim seemed.

"It's all arranged," Kim said.

Sara looked puzzled and raised her hands to indicate confusion. "Arranged?"

"The Side Door Café reopens next Sunday. Mr. & Mrs. Sullivan — the owners — had the whole place inspected. Everything is fine."

Sara shook her head. "Slow down!" *Slow.* "What are you talking about?"

Keesha tapped Kim's arm. "We don't have time now, Kim. We have to get up to my mother's office. She's waiting to drive us home."

"Okay. okay. I have a modeling assignment in half an hour, too. Anyway, I asked the Sullivans about poetry readings in ASL instead of spoken English. They think it's a wonderful idea, especially for this coming Sunday — something different for the re-opening.

"I told them you'd start everything. If you don't have your own poetry, you can sign somebody else's."

No way! No thanks!

Kim looked at Keesha for a translation. Keesha shrugged. "You can't just throw this on Sara. She doesn't want to do it!"

"Sara's mad at me? I lined up something I thought would be fun. She doesn't understand," Kim said.

Hearing people! One of the constant annoyances for Sara was being referred to in the third person as if she were on the moon instead of right there. Sara tapped Kim's shoulder angrily. "Talk to me. I can understand you. Yes, I'm angry." She scrunched her fingers in front of her face. *Angry.* "You have to ask first. Everything in life can't be the way you want it."

"How was I supposed to know you'd have such a tantrum?"

Sara glared, then sighed. Kim seemed always to be racing from one thing to another, whether it was class, or an appointment, or a modeling session. It didn't take long to discover that trying to keep up was exhausting.

Kim pouted. "We could get a good group together — all your friends. Steve, too, of course. I'm sure he'll want to be there if he's not working."

Steve? That was it! She still had a crush on Steve!

*　　*　　*

That night Sara was still distracted. She had too much homework to stew over Kim Roth, but as she sat at her computer in the den, her mind continued to wander back to the afternoon's conversation. It was hard to fight with hearing people. Even when she argued with Steve, she couldn't always be sure if he understood what she was trying to say. With someone as headstrong as Kim, she wasn't sure if anything got through.

The desk lamp began to blink, indicating that someone was ringing the doorbell downstairs in the lobby. To confirm it, Tuck trotted to her and put his paws in her lap.

I know, she signed and stroked him. Steve was home. He would get the door. She was about to force herself back to the assignment, when her brother appeared in the doorway.

Look who's here, he signed.

Kimberly Roth appeared behind him, flushed and wide-eyed. Her makeup was heavy, but perfectly applied, and her light hair was done up in a sophisticated knot. From her manicured nails to her designer jeans, Kim looked perfect.

Steve looked stunned.

Chapter 7

Sara watched in confusion as Steve told Kim to sit on the couch. He left, then reappeared with a glass of water which Kim sipped self-consciously.

"Start at the beginning," Steve said.

Sara frowned and moved closer to read their lips.

Kim took a deep breath. "Okay, I was driving by on my way home from the photo shoot. Spring prom dresses, if you can believe it. We're always a season ahead. Look at me. I haven't even taken off my makeup. I need to get home ... English paper and Spanish quiz tomorrow. I'm so sorry. I'm probably interrupting." She glanced quickly from brother to sister. Sara did not get the impression that Kim was sorry, or that she minded interrupting.

"She thought she was . . . *being followed. Dark car,*" Steve added in his combined English and sign.

Kim nodded. "The modeling shoot was at the Montgomery Studios on Station Street. They're in the loft over the old Radley train station. You know the shops downstairs, restaurants. Big safe parking lot. I wasn't worried at all, but somebody followed me out of the parking lot and all the way down North Avenue."

"Did you get a license number? Can you describe the car?" *Car number?*

"No number. I couldn't see it. The car was big and dark. Mostly I saw headlights in my rearview mirror."

"North Avenue has streetlights. Couldn't you see the color or the make of the vehicle behind you?"

"Well, no. No, I couldn't."

"Where were the headlights in relation to your car? High like a four-wheel drive vehicle? Medium sized? Low like a sports car?"

"Medium. Medium, like a normal-size car."

"You said the car was big." *Car was big.* He glanced at Sara to see if she was following the conversation.

Kim blushed. "It could have been big . . . a big medium-sized car. I was afraid it would follow me all the way home, so I came here."

Sara tapped Steve's arm. *We aren't anywhere near her way home. North Avenue Police Station is right down the road from that studio.*

"You must have driven right past the police station," Steve added to Kim. "You should have stopped right there and asked for help."

"I was so rattled . . ."

"Why would someone follow you?"

"Why?" Kim moved to the edge of the couch as Sara strained to understand the conversation.

"What I mean is, could it have been a bunch of teenagers, who, maybe, saw you leaving the studio and thought you were cute? Sort of obnoxious harassment. . . . Or would you have any reason to think someone might have more sinister motives?"

"Motives? No."

Kim's demeanor surprised Sara. Rather than relaxing her, Steve's interest and questions made her fidget.

For Sara, Steve spoke and signed, *"Police Station. Why don't I drive you to my station and you can file a report? Fourth Precinct at Penn Street's not far from here."*

At that, Kim stood up. "Oh no, really, I'm fine. I can't describe who it was, or even identify the car. I just thought I'd . . . stop by . . . tell you . . . I don't know. It was probably nothing."

"Are your parents home?"

"Yes, for once."

"Good. Tell them, right away."

Sara studied Steve as he spoke. He was doing a good job of staying professional, despite what she knew he was thinking. After an awkward pause, he stood up. "You were right to stop by if you were concerned, but your parents need to know, and next time, go to the nearest police station."

"I'm sixteen. You make me feel like I'm in kindergarten."

"Then I've done my job. Believe it or not, it's the same advice you learned as a kid."

"That's it? Tell a grown-up? Gee, thanks." *Thanks,* Kim signed to both of them.

Sara raised her eyebrows at the sarcasm in her friend's expression and the exasperation in her brother's.

Steve tapped his watch in a reminder that there was homework to finish, then got the leash to take Tuck for his walk. "Make sure you walk Kim out to her car when she leaves," he added.

Kim looked disappointed as he left. Reluctantly she turned to Sara. "I did stop by to apologize to you, too." She seemed to regain her confidence. "You were really mad at me this afternoon." She circled her heart. *Sorry.*

Sara shrugged. "I didn't mean to get so angry. I just don't want to sign at the café."

"Maybe another time?"

Sara signed. *No!*

*   *   *

"Your brother is amazing. He even cares if you do your homework," Kim said ten minutes later as she let Sara walk her to the car. She turned off her alarm and opened the door.

Sara wrinkled her nose. "My brother cares too much about most things in my life. It feels like he has to know every detail. This car stuff won't help, believe me."

"How could anybody care too much?" Her glance was distant. Kimberly Roth had been an aloof mystery, a glamorous classmate many of the others left alone. She had a reputation for being spoiled and headstrong. Sara couldn't argue with the latter, but the more she got to know Kim, the more she wondered about her being spoiled. It was beginning to seem like neglected was a better word for describing her.

Sara stayed in the courtyard long enough to watch Kim's car round the bend at the traffic light and head out toward Riverside Drive. No mysterious cars raced around the corner after her on two wheels. No vehicle followed at a discreet distance. The only questionable character lurking in the shadows was Tuck sniffing his way home along the curb with Steve at the other end of his leash.

Sara's brother looked lost in thought. *K-I-M gone?*

Yes. "We both had work to finish for school." She made Kim's name sign to remind him.

"Obviously she made it to her car safely. I gather no one tried to run either of you over."

Sara raised an eyebrow at his sarcasm. *No, but I'm sure she wished I'd been you.*

Me?

Don't tell you haven't noticed!

Steve tapped his mouth to indicate that what he had to say needed concentration to understand and was important. He spoke and signed. *"One of the truest things Dad taught me about police work was to trust instincts. Sometimes that's all you have to go by."*

"I know. It worked with me, with all that mystery over his death. Things just felt wrong."

"*Okay.*" He glanced around the parking lot and shook his head. "*Tonight things felt wrong. Just as you said.*" He lifted his shoulders. "*I think Kim made up the whole story about being followed.*"

Chapter 8

Sara was slow to agree, but she finally nodded. "She does things that seem like showing off, but I think she's looking for attention." *Attention. I know she's a model and everything, but it's almost like she's lonely.*

Lonely? With those looks?

She scares boys away, Keesha says. Too glamorous. "Maybe tonight she just wanted you to pay attention to her. You could see by the way she reacted that she never expected you to ask her to tell her story to the police department."

"But I am the police department."

"Yes, but you're also my handsome, glamorous brother." She glanced around her. "Kim really is worried about her car."

Steve frowned. *Say again.*

"I wasn't going to tell you, but Saturday morning when Kim stayed over and her car was here . . . I walked Tuck . . . *a car came through this lot, right over to the door . . .*"

Steve straightened up in alarm. *"You mean it happened again? You didn't tell me?"*

"Not followed," Sara explained. "I didn't tell you because I knew you'd overreact." *Understand?*

Yes! "I am not overreacting. Did you get a clear look?"

Sara brought her index finger and thumb together to indicate a little look. "Dark. Got a glimpse of the driver. No passenger, no woman like the first time." *Couldn't see.* "He nearly sideswiped John O'Connor and me, then left." She pointed to the spot.

Steve nodded. "Like the night before, out at Winchester Commons. We get calls about kids parking out there. Lovers' Lane. Hangout. Speeding, too."

"I know. That's why we figured it might

just be bad driving. It was too fast to be anything else. Don't forget I've been followed before. I know what it feels like. This second time . . ." She shook her head. *Really, forget about it. I wasn't worried about me, just about Kim's car getting scratched.*

"Big worry. Fancy car."

Very rich parents.

"No kidding. I didn't know till she gave me her father's name at the hospital. David Roth. Major power broker. Investments, mergers . . . very busy."

"Too busy for Kim."

"Has Kim broken up with any boyfriends recently? Anybody upset with her?"

"Like stalkers or something? No. According to Liz and Keesha, Kim hardly has time to date, let alone get serious enough to break somebody's heart. After classes she's mostly modeling or working out." The breeze circled her ankles. "Let's go in."

Cold. Sara signed it to herself as she snapped off the lights in the empty apartment. Steve was on duty again. She was uneasy in the big, silent rooms.

She went down the hall to her bedroom and tried to finish her homework, but each time she glanced up from her desk, she met the magazine cutout of Kim she'd tacked to her bulletin board. She got up and walked to the window. Seven floors below, she had a view of the Thurston Court entrance. The spot where Kim had parked her car was empty. She wondered what kind of reaction Kim had expected from Steve. Deep down, Sara had to admit that she thought Kimberly Roth was capable of making up a story about being followed just for the attention.

Her thoughts scattered as Tuck nudged the back of her legs. No lights had blinked, indicating the door or the phone. She patted his head, but as she turned back to the window, he nudged her again. She patted his head again and he relaxed. Silly, she said to herself, but her heart hammered.

To rid herself of the jitters, she called Bret on the TTY. She wasn't about to admit that she'd called because the empty apartment was upsetting her. Instead she pretended she'd forgotten whether he was working Saturday night. He reminded her that he was, and after idle chat, they made another early date for Sunday night. When she hung up she ruffled Tuck's fur. *Scaring me was worth it, you silly dog,* she signed to herself.

But she wished Steve were home.

Chapter 9

I hate Sunday dates. They always have to be short. School night; homework. Yuk.

Bret laughed at Sara's signing as they huddled against the autumn wind on their way to the Side Door Café's take-out counter.

Sara stopped at the edge of the patio and pointed to the empty space where the awning had been fastened to the brick wall. *That's where the bolts were loosened. Steve says they still have no suspects; no motive, just evidence that they were loosened, maybe even pulled out.*

How about insurance fraud?

The police are convinced the owners are telling the truth. They swear they would never put people at risk just to collect some money. It doesn't make sense. If I —

Bret grabbed her hands between his, then dropped them to sign. *I'm sorry it fell on you and your friends, but don't even think about trying to find out why . . . or who . . . or anything else!*

Sara smiled, but she shivered as she reached the spot where her table had been. Bret kissed her, put his arm around her, and walked with her down the alley and through the entrance.

As usual the café was packed with students, and a glimpse of familiar red hair caught Sara's eye. Liz Martinson and Kim Roth were working their way to the door.

"I thought you weren't coming here tonight," Kim said as she reached them.

"Not performing here. We're just picking up some hot chocolate and dessert," Sara replied.

You okay? Sara signed to Kim. "You seem down."

"I'm fine." She looked at her feet. "I don't expect you to believe me, but some guy tried to pick me up when I got my car. He was at the shed and pretended his car wouldn't start and asked for a lift. You know, 'Where are you going? Gee, what a coincidence, so am I' kind of stuff."

Sara frowned as she tried to read Kim's lips and signed, *Say again.*

Kim spoke slower.

"You told him you were coming here?"

"No! Only that I had to pick up a friend. Liz was pacing outside by the time I got to her place."

"Where is the guy now?"

"Who knows. What he didn't realize was that my bedroom window looks down on the parking area and I saw his car drive up about five minutes before I left to get mine. His car was running just fine. I told him to call a mechanic . . . for his brain."

"It wasn't the same one?"

Kim waved off the question and shook her head. "I thought of that, too."

"With your looks, happens all the time, I bet," Sara replied.

Kim shrugged. "By everybody but your brother."

Sara said, "You did make up that car chase Wednesday night, didn't you?"

Color suddenly blotted Kim's cheeks. "Does he think so?"

Sara shrugged. "He's a cop." *Cop.* "Can't fool him."

"I was stupid, right?"

"Not stupid. But if tonight was real, it's a good thing you're taking Liz home. Do you want Bret and me to follow, too, just to be safe?"

"No. That was hours ago and I am safe. He was just a guy looking for a date. That's life, isn't it? All the attention in the world from people I don't want."

The four of them walked to the parking lot together. Bret laughed as Kim signed the alphabet for him. She was getting smooth. *I practice,* she signed.

"Speaking of which," Liz interrupted as she handed over a three-ring binder, "we never got to Spanish homework tonight. Promise you'll bring it to school in the morning. I'm dead without it."

Kim nodded and took a deep breath. "Smell the bakery? Vanilla tonight. Let's meet here tomorrow after school. We'll call it ASL hour. An hour, no speaking, only signing. It'll be fun . . . the talk of school. The more we learn to sign, the easier it'll be for Sara."

Sara kept her surprise to herself. *Thanks.*

"Look, Kim, if it's really so important, I guess we could all meet here a little after five," Bret said.

Sara agreed. A friend who was interested in learning to communicate with her language was important, but she still had the feeling that it was far more crucial to Kim. If this was her way of making — or keeping — friends it was fine with her. "I'll take the car to school," Sara added. *Drive. Pick Bret up after rowing.*

I'll meet you on the steps of the library, he signed back.

"Then it's settled. I have to see a guy about a new modeling assignment. I can do it after school and I'll be finished by then, too. We'll meet back here. It'll be fun and we'll all be home in time for dinner." Kim gave each of them a satisfied smile. She opened the back door of her car and pulled some sweaters from a pile of clothes. "Samples from a shoot. I can't wait to get home and try them on. Want some?"

"Me?"

"Really." She held up three.

Sara took two. "Not my style," she said and she handed back a red-striped sweater.

"There might be others that fit, too. I haven't had time to go through them," Kim replied. Proudly she pointed at Sara and swept her hand to the right. *Go to it!*

Thank you, Sara replied as she left with Bret.

Kim Roth was absent. Her seat stayed empty through Monday morning homeroom, then English. After fourth period, Sara stopped Liz in the hall to confirm it. Liz nodded.

"What about your Spanish notes?"

Liz shrugged and dodged a classmate. "All I know is that she's not here. She was supposed to give her oral report in history. No show. Maybe she hadn't finished working on it and called in sick. Kim's always cramming at the last minute. Her parents both work. Even when they're home, they leave before she does. Who's to know if she stayed home? There wouldn't be anybody else home except the housekeeper. If she arrives and Kim's acting sick, or like she's supposed to be home, she wouldn't think anything about it. Wish I had it that easy."

Sara signed *telephone*. Liz shrugged. "Okay. During study hall next period. Get a pass to the bathroom. I'll meet you at the pay phone across from the gym. We'll call and give her a hard time."

Sara signed that she understood.

Fifty minutes later, Sara leaned against the wall outside the gym as Liz punched in the phone number for Kim Roth's townhouse. Sara positioned herself so she could read Liz's lips, and waited. After a pause, Liz spoke into the receiver. She frowned. Suddenly she put her free hand over her other ear and nodded toward the gym.

Sara turned and scowled at the open gym doors and the class hurling itself through aerobic exercises, obviously making enough noise that Liz had to turn away. Sara tapped her foot and waited. When she turned back, Liz had hung up.

"What happened?" Sara asked.

"Her father actually answered the phone — in the middle of a work day."

Sara pantomimed yanking up the phone and Liz nodded. "Waiting for an important call. Working from home."

"Maybe," Liz replied. "Since I was stuck with Mr. Roth, I had to think of something, so I said we were calling to see how Kim was feeling."

Sara frowned as she tried to interpret her friend's hurried speech. *Slow down.* "What did he say?"

"He said Kim left on a modeling assignment. He said he called the school office. They know."

Sara nodded that she understood the conversation. "When is she coming back?"

"'A few days,' Mr. Roth said."

Where is she? "Did you ask where she is?"

"He said she's in New York. Mr. Roth said

he'd tell Kim wc said hello when she calls in tonight."

Say again.

N-Y. Liz finger spelled, then made the sign for *camera.*

"Lucky Kim," Sara said.

Chapter 10

New York. Sara sat in study hall and doodled N Y all over the margin of her loose-leaf paper. She ignored the scrutiny of the room proctor and stared into space. New York City was hours from Radley, even by plane. Kim had said she was to see someone about a new assignment, but that was supposed to be after school. Today, in Radley, not in New York. New York! Kim often talked of her independence, but Sara found it amazing that her parents would let her fly off at a moment's notice, let alone work by herself.

Sara searched for logic. Kim's agent must be with her. Maybe a chaperon had been assigned from the agency. Sara didn't know any more about modeling than Kim knew about ASL. She opened her biology book so the proctor would stop glaring. She imagined Kim posing in Central Park with the leaves blazing with fall color . . . and her dress adjusted with clothespins all the way up the back.

It doesn't make sense. That afternoon Sara leaned against her car and signed to Liz and Keesha in the parking lot of the Shelter Island boathouse. "Kim would let one of us know if her plans had changed."

"Not if this were last minute. We didn't get home till after nine last night," Liz replied.

"But she wanted us all back at the café tonight. I can understand that she might not be comfortable calling me because of the relay operator, but she would have called one of you before she left." *Big news, big surprise. New York!*

Liz shrugged. "The only thing that gripes me is the Spanish. I got in big trouble for not having my notebook. You know Kim. New York is big stuff, even to her. It's her dream."

N.-Y. Kim's dream, she signed for Sara's benefit. "She got the chance and jumped at it, that's all. Never mind how it affects us."

Sara was dealing with her own annoyance. "Well, it's rude."

Liz turned to Keesha and the two of them spoke rapidly.

Sara tapped Keesha's shoulder harder than she should have. "Don't you be rude. Can't read your lips."

Keesha circled her heart. "Sorry. Really. We were just saying Kim does this kind of thing. Sort of jumps from hot to cold. Last night the café idea was important, but something better came along. So that's the end of us, typical of Kim."

Sara was tired. Before they'd left for crew practice she'd had Keesha phone the library to tell Bret there was no meeting at the café. With nothing left to say, she asked if either of them wanted a ride home. Keesha was meeting her mother at school; Liz said yes.

Sara watched the road carefully as she drove. She was sorry she'd snapped at Keesha and Liz. She tried to soothe her frustration at not being able to understand conversations by reminding herself that she'd only been back in the hearing world since the end of summer. At Edgewood School for the Deaf she never missed conversations, never felt like an outsider.

She supposed Kim Roth felt like an outsider, too, in her own way. That was why she was always trying so hard; why the café after school had been so important; why she lied to Steve. Sara gripped the wheel. And yet she had just gone off, never thinking of their date.

Sara stopped her reverie as she slowed for a yellow light. She admired Riverside and the stately turn-of-the-century houses that lined the avenue. Like Kim, Liz Martinson lived in Radley's most fashionable section of the city. Sara pulled into the Martinsons' driveway and put the car in park.

Liz smiled. "It's a chocolate afternoon," she said as she put her face to the open window and smelled the cookie factory. "I'll bet New York doesn't smell this good." She stared straight ahead at the oversized garage at the end of the driveway, then turned to Sara. "Last year Kim got angry at her parents for never being around. She came over and stayed in our apartment — old chauffeur's quarters over the garage — to see how long it would take till they missed her. I didn't even tell my parents. I snuck her food. Everything. It was fun till my mother saw shadows one night and thought somebody had broken in. They called the police."

"Do you think she'd run away again?"

"Her father said she's in New York. So she is!"

"I guess so," Sara replied.

Five minutes later Sara was at the bend in Riverside Drive. Abruptly she turned through the gates to Winchester Commons, and followed the narrow lane that meandered among the townhouses. As she approached the parking shed, she automatically looked at the parked cars. Kim's car wasn't in her spot. Bay seven was empty. The same spot where she'd nearly been hit, the same spot Kim said someone had tried to pick her up.

If Kim were really in New York there was a good chance the car was at the airport. Sara shook her head and continued around the bend to the Roth townhouse. She parked at the curb and sat while her heart raced under her crew team jacket. This was crazy. What if no one understood her? What if they got angry at her for snooping? After a deep breath she got out of the car.

Halfway up the walk, a face appeared at the window in the door. It was a man with dark hair and horn-rimmed glasses. He was tall enough that Sara could see the suspenders over the shoulders of his dress shirt. His eyebrows knit as she approached and he spoke, then turned his head and disappeared. She read his lips: *Who the hell is this?* he'd said.

Everything felt weird. She looked back in the direction of the parking shed. What if somebody were holding Kim and her family hostage in their townhouse? Maybe whoever Liz had spoken to from the school phone said Kim was in New York so nobody would suspect anything.

Chills were beginning to raise the hair at the nape of her neck. She pulled her jacket tighter and took a step forward. As she walked, the front door opened. At close range she recognized the man from the photos inside. So much for my imagination, Sara thought. Nerves made her blush and her palms dampen, but she stuck out her hand. "Mr. Roth. I'm Sara Howell. I was with Kim last Friday night when the awning collapsed at the Side Door Café."

Sara tapped her chest. "My brother Steve called you at the hotel for medical information." She waited, anticipated the quizzical look she always got when someone listened to her muffled voice, and realized she was deaf.

David Roth nodded. "Yes. Yes, of course. You're the friend who's teaching Kim sign language. Kim practices on me a little. The book she bought is right out back in the family room." He spoke slowly as if she were a child.

Sara swallowed her irritation and tapped her chest. "I called with Liz Martinson this morning from school."

"Yes. Howell. Your brother — who called me from the hospital — is the police officer?"

Sara nodded.

"As I told the school, Kim's out of town for a few days. Quite a glamorous life. It was too good an opportunity to pass up." He smiled casually.

"Last night she said she had to see someone about a new assignment. Was this the one? Did Todd Russell, her agent, go with her?" Sara asked. Gut instinct, gut instinct. She thought of her father and imagined what his reaction would be as he watched David Roth's nervous demeanor.

"Her agent? Yes. Yes, Todd flew out with her. Now if you'll excuse me . . ."

Think! She stepped closer. "The reason I stopped by is because I need my Spanish notebook. Kim borrowed it last night and was going to bring it to school this morning. I hope my Spanish isn't in New York."

"I'm afraid I wouldn't know." Mr. Roth shook his head with annoyance.

As they spoke, Sara glanced behind him, into the foyer. A figure was barely visible through an arched doorway at the back of the entrance hall. He was sitting on the stool at the kitchen counter where she and Keesha had eaten pizza with Kim a week earlier.

Kim's poodle trotted across the room and as Sara watched, the man left the room. Something else caught her eye. Kim's backpack was leaning against the easy chair in the family area behind the stools. The poodle sniffed it and lay down.

Chapter 11

Sara smiled apologetically to Mr. Roth. "Kim's backpack's right where she usually leaves it, by her dog."

He turned around, then back to her. "So it is."

"That's too bad," Sara continued. "I guess she forgot it. That fouls up her assignments while she's away. Would you mind if I see if my notebook's there?" Without waiting, she crossed the foyer and entered the kitchen.

She could feel him follow, probably issuing directives at her. She grinned. Sometimes deafness came in handy.

The moment Sara got back in the car, she leaned her forehead on the steering wheel.

The man who'd left the kitchen had been standing just inside the laundry room, unaware that his shadow showed clearly on the floor. She looked at the passenger seat. The notebook hadn't been opened. It was still sealed on the side with tape so the loose papers wouldn't fall out, the way she'd seen it in Liz's hand at the café. Kim either never got to it, or she got the call about New York and decided it wasn't worth handing in the past assignment.

Sara shook her head, more confused than ever. She knew from Keesha's mother, the head of Lower School, what a strict policy the school had with kids who miss a lot. Work had to be done in advance. Old work, like the Spanish, had to be completed.

Sara was getting a funny feeling in the pit of her stomach. Something wasn't right, and it was times like these when she missed her father the most.

Kim was organized. She kept a planner. Had she been in such a hurry that she would have forgotten her backpack? And who was the other person in the laundry room? David Roth had been nervous. Sara shook her head.

She knew body language the way hearing people knew regional accents. The big-shot power broker had been sweating.

Kim didn't take the ASL book she was so excited about. She practices while she's working because she spends so much time waiting around, Sara remembered. Her blue eyes were wide and troubled. Maybe Kim fought with her parents and ran away — maybe just long enough to make them pay attention. How many times had she complained that they didn't care about her, or even have a clue about what was going on in her life. Liz had just admitted to hiding her in the Martinson apartment.

Sara didn't like the feelings churning around inside. She slid the car into gear and came up with the next plan.

The airport was a twenty-minute drive each way. A quick search for KIMZ and she'd be back at Thurston Court in time for a late dinner. Sara laughed. If she had a plane to catch, there was no way her brother would just tell her to be on her way. Steve was so protective, he'd probably pack himself into her luggage.

She pulled from the Commons out onto Riverside Drive and drove in stop-and-go traffic. She crossed over the river and into Hillsboro on the Shadow Point Bridge. As she drove along the infamous span, she wondered if there would ever be a day when the bridge and the park below it wouldn't remind her of her father and the corruption that had caused his death.

The Packard County Airport was across the river and straight out a four-lane highway built expressly to move airport traffic. She joined other cars and hotel shuttles from Radley and Hillsboro. As she checked her side-view mirror before passing a delivery truck, a red car came up behind her and made the same maneuver. She pulled back into the lane, in front of the truck. The red car stayed in the passing lane, matching her speed. When she finally pulled ahead, the red car moved in behind her.

Twenty minutes later Sara had her blinker on for the airport exit. The car behind her had fallen back among many others, but as those vehicles going in her direction left the highway, the red car joined them. Sara kept her glance jumping: ahead, rearview mirror, sideview mirror, despite the fact that there was nothing unusual about two cars taking Riverside Drive, the Shadow Point Bridge, and the highway to the airport.

On overhead rails, color-coded signs made it easy to follow the lanes leading to the airport parking areas. SHORT-TERM PARKING was to her left. She stopped at the gate, took a ticket and entered on the lowest level. For the next fifteen minutes Sara drove her car slowly down one parking aisle and up the next, then up the ramp until she'd covered all three floors. When she thought to look again for the red car, it was gone.

Although there were a few cars that matched Kim's color or the model, nothing was an exact match. There wasn't a KIMZ license plate on any of them.

When she was sure she had checked every space, Sara drove back out and handed the attendant her ticket. He waved her through when she explained that she hadn't parked. Then, just to be sure, Sara repeated the search in the regular parking lot. It was smaller, designed for those who left their cars for a week or longer. Still no KIMZ, no sleek black import.

She left with the low sun in her eyes as she drove the wide loop that made up the airport exit, and headed back to the county highway. At the yield sign she automatically looked from the overpass to a six-lane road below. The red car had just pulled from the ramp into traffic and was heading back to Radley.

Nothing about this feels right, Sara thought. Chills returned.

Thirty minutes later, Sara was back in Radley and heading for the college district. She pulled up in front of Bret's home, a brick three-story house at the edge of the Radley University campus where Bret's parents were members of the faculty. As she left the car, she spotted Bret as he got off the city bus at the corner. Sara ran the half block and threw her arms around his neck.

Bret swung her around and laughed before she landed back on her feet. *I'm glad to see you, too! Long day at the library. Sorry Kim had other plans tonight. I could have used a few minutes at the Side Door. How was crew practice?*

Forget crew! Sara's hands flew. She started with the phone call to the Roths' from school and didn't stop until she explained the visit to Winchester Commons. All the while Bret's animated features grew from curious, to concerned, to angry.

I don't even have to ask if Steve knows what you're doing.

This isn't about Steve; it's about Kim, she replied.

She's in New York. Her own father said so. A forgotten backpack and Spanish notes don't change that, Bret signed.

No car. Her car isn't at the townhouse and it's not in any of the parking areas at the airport.

Bret's eyes widened in alarm. *You've been out to the airport? Did Keesha and Liz go, too?*

No. They don't think anything's wrong. Sara stopped as she realized what a hole she was digging for herself.

You drove out there by yourself? Sara, this is stupid and risky!

If nothing's happened to Kim, how come I was followed out there, all the way to the parking garage?

Bret drove his hand through his hair. *Who followed you?*

Sara shrugged. *A red car. That's all I know.*

You can't just run around doing stuff like this. You were probably followed because you're cute and alone and —

I came over here because I thought you'd understand, Sara shot back.

Bret shook his head. *I understand that you're taking chances and jumping to a lot of conclusions.*

You're acting more like my brother every minute.

Maybe he needs help getting you to use common sense, Bret shot back.

Sara wiped angry tears off her cheeks. *Sorry I came over here. I have to drop the notebook back at Liz's.* She turned on her heel. Bret didn't stop her.

Chapter 12

Kimberly Roth. Sara fought her own anger as she knocked at the Martinsons' kitchen door. Liz opened it and the aroma of cinnamon and apples wafted into the driveway as Sara held the Spanish notebook out.

"What on earth?"

Sara explained.

Liz turned it over. "I taped it to keep the papers from falling out. She never opened it."

"Doesn't that say something?"

Liz was annoyed now. "Sara, it says she got a last-minute deal in New York and didn't have time. I admit this Kim business is a whole lot more interesting than Mr. Hagstrom's biology assignment, and the rough draft of my Spanish essay, but that's what

I'll be doing tonight." She held up her note-book. "Thanks to dear old Kim I'm a day be-hind already. Sorry." She circled her heart. "You look so disappointed."

Sara was drained from her fight with Bret and not about to get into another argument. *I'm okay.* "I guess I'll see you tomorrow."

Tomorrow, Liz signed back.

The minute Keesha opened her apartment door, Sara regretted having knocked. The Fletchers were at their dinner table. It had been cinnamon and apples at Liz's, and now the homey aroma of chicken filled the hall. As quickly as she could, Sara explained what she'd discovered.

Keesha nodded and congratulated her on having the nerve to go to the Roths' by her-self, but she wasn't any more convinced than Bret or Liz by the notebook or the missing car. "It's not really missing just because you didn't find it," Keesha said with her hand on Sara's arm. "Sara, you're imagining things. Forget it."

Sara shrugged maybe-you're-right, and

signed *good night*. Keesha gave her the high sign before she turned back to her dinner.

Sara's heart ached. Keesha had a teenage brother and parents and a home-cooked dinner. Steve was the only family Sara had and he was as apt to be at the police station as waiting for her. Her grief had dulled since school had started, but it welled up again and mixed with the frustration the day had brought.

She unlocked her own door, grateful that Tuck was already in the foyer, tail wagging. The lamp on the hall table operated on a timer that snapped it on at four P.M. The single light barely illuminated the entrance. Alone again. There would be yet another note from her brother on the kitchen counter. She dropped her backpack and went to read it and got a mental flash of Kim's kitchen counter. A man had been there when she'd arrived. He had stepped into the laundry room when she entered the kitchen. Hiding? Sara wondered. She sighed. Keesha or Liz or Bret would probably say he was just some houseguest pulling his own clothes out of the dryer.

Sara picked up the sheet of paper. Maybe it was the holes in her own life that made her so concerned with Kim's. She shrugged and deciphered her brother's familiar scrawl:

> Sara —
> Working late again. If you don't
> have too much homework, grab us
> some dinner at the Penn Street
> Deli and bring it over. Call if you
> can't. Otherwise, I'll see you at the
> station.
>
> > XX Steve

Her brother was trying to be all things to her and she loved him for it, but it wasn't the same as what Keesha, Bret, and Liz, and even Kim had.

Dark soon; not much left of Daylight Saving Time. Sara dropped her bookbag in her room, but didn't bother to change from the sweats she'd worn to crew practice. She snapped on Tuck's leash, led him down the elevator and onto the street. In a few weeks the sun would be gone by this time in the evening. The October light was low already as the sun sank behind the commercial building west of Thurston Court.

Sara headed toward Penn Street, a healthy fifteen-minute walk. Wherever Kim was, at least she had one friend concerned about her.

Normally Sara loved this time of day. Every bus that stopped let off riders anxious to end the workday. Many of the shops between the apartment and the precinct station were small and bustling. Cleaners, groceries, shoe repair and pharmacies catered to men and women doing last-minute errands on their way home.

During the walk Sara conjured up occupations for the anonymous commuters, a game she'd played as a child with her family to practice signing with them. Tuck skirted two women in business suits and running shoes. *Olympic track stars, after a television interview.* A guy about her brother's age with a ponytail and earring stood at the bus stop with a rectangular package. *Artist, on his way to the gallery.*

She caught sight of a man in the doorway

of the corner laundry watching her as he sipped a cup of coffee. She slid Tuck's leash from her wrist back into her palm, and shoved her free hand into her pocket self-consciously. As he lifted the Styrofoam cup to his mouth, she noticed that his pinky finger was missing.

S-P-Y, she finger spelled in her pocket. *F-O-R-E-I-G-N A-G-E-N-T. Lost his finger in a terrorist attack.* The man glanced at Tuck as she passed. Why?

Sara gripped Tuck's leash and fought the flutter of chills between her shoulder blades as if she were being watched. Mr. Hagstrom's biology assignment wouldn't stand a chance if she kept this up.

She couldn't get rid of the tingling and fought the urge to spin around and face the demons her imagination was designing. Crowded street. Bright lights. She was being ridiculous.

As usual the Penn Street Delicatessen smelled delicious, even out on the sidewalk. She dropped the loop of Tuck's leash over the parking meter at the curb. He knew the routine and sat obediently to wait while she shopped. Over the years the Patrone family had expanded their delicatessen to more of a small grocery store. It catered to the late hours of the local police and firefighters up the street, as well as the commuters and neighbors.

The deli was bustling. She wrote her order on a piece of paper from the small spiral notebook she kept in her purse. Emilio Patrone smiled and nodded as he went to fill her order.

During her first year at Edgewood, her father had been lead detective on an investigation that involved neighborhood robberies and the wounding of Emilio Patrone in a break-in. Lieutenant Howell had solved the case. When he wrote to Sara about it, she was so proud, she'd signed his entire letter to her seventh-grade class.

"Your brother, hungry tonight?" the grandfatherly Emilio asked as he wrapped the oversized submarine sandwiches.

"Always hungry," she replied. It felt good to smile. *"Always."*

There was no charge. Although this had

been going on since her father's funeral, Sara blushed as the older man refused her money. Emilio's smile was kind, but determined.

He tapped the old scar on his shoulder. "No argue. No charge, not for you, not for Stefano. Not ever. You need anything, you come to the Patrones."

Thank you.

You're welcome, he signed back proudly.

Affection warmed her as she took the bulging bag that would be supper. She turned to leave and faltered as she reached the door. The man without a pinky was on the sidewalk. He held the door for her, nodded, and crossed to the counter. Sara didn't realize she'd been holding her breath until she reached Tuck at the parking meter. She had to gasp to catch her breath as her retriever stood up and wagged his tail.

Had Mr. No Pinky been waiting for her?

Sara! Stop this! she told herself.

The police station that had been such a part of her life was quiet. Two squad cars were parked in the front. The desk sergeant waved as she entered and pantomimed that her brother was upstairs starving. Sara smiled. She was as comfortable in the Fourth Precinct station as she was in her own apartment. It made her feel good that a photograph of her father hung in a place of honor behind the front desk.

She and Tuck climbed the stairs to the small two-desk office Steve shared with detectives who worked other shifts. He was on the phone, but waved her in and hung up, then motioned that they would eat in the kitchen area at the end of the hall. The Interrogation Room door was open and a handful of officers sat around the desk looking at papers. They waved, too.

Quiet night, she signed.

Just the way we like it. He spread the contents of the bag on paper plates. "Good choice. Did Rocco or Emilio let you pay?"

Sara shook her head.

Steve smiled. "I don't argue anymore. It makes the Patrones feel like they're helping us, and it makes me feel good that they thought so much of Dad."

Sara paused as Lieutenant Rosemary Marino came in to use the coffee machine.

Over the years she had worked with father and son, and was a Howell family friend as well as the community liaison officer for the precinct. She filled her mug and greeted them. As she left, Steve took a huge bite of his deli sandwich, but he signaled Sara and signed with his mouth full. *She reminds me. I guess your friend was careless with that fancy car.*

What friend?

Steve motioned after Lieutenant Marino with a nod of his head. He looked at his fingers and tried: *K-I-M.* He added *K, Camera* the way she'd taught him. *Her car was towed away. Showed up on the police report this morning.*

Chapter 13

A knot tightened in Sara's stomach. *Kim's car was towed?*

Parked in tow zone. He shrugged his shoulders. *She should have been more careful, especially after she was so afraid somebody was out to steal it.*

Towed! How do you know? Where?

Steve paused at Sara's confusion, finally swallowed and took a sip of coffee. "You know Rosemary's hobby — she collects the names people use on their vanity license plates. Copies them down when the plates come over the printouts of stolen car reports or the tow sheets from the RPD lot. She has them on the bulletin board over her desk. Officers even add to the list when they see an unusual one on the street."

Steve! Get to the point!

*Kim's car. I thought you would know —
from school. Maybe after all that nonsense
about being followed, she was too embarrassed to tell you it had been towed.* He
looked startled and wiggled his fingers, their
signal that he was unsure about how to sign
the rest. "This morning I saw KIMZ on Rosemary's list. Obviously I remembered the
plate — not to mention that hot car — "

Where did they find the car?

Steve shrugged. *Don't know.* "Rosemary
said the plate came through on the printout of
recovered vehicles. That means it had been
towed and was at our lot." He put his hand on
her shoulder. "You look stunned." He circled
his heart. *Sorry.* "The night Kim tried to convince me she'd been followed, she seemed to
like being the center of attention. Did she
ever admit that she'd made up the story?"

Sara blushed into her scalp.

Steve pointed at her. "She did make it all
up, didn't she?"

"Not this time."

He frowned. *Say again.*

Sara wasn't paying attention. "How do we get details?"

"Whoa! Why not ask Kim? I thought she would milk real news like this for all it's worth."

No Kim. "Kim wasn't in school." As clearly as she could, Sara told Steve about her day and the odd visit at Winchester Commons with David Roth. She stopped short of mentioning her trip to the airport. "Her father wants everyone to believe that Kim is in New York on a modeling assignment. But I don't. Don't you see? Her backpack is here. Her car was towed because it was dumped somewhere. Deserted. Something's happened to Kim!"

Steve shook his head and frowned to indicate that he thought he hadn't understood her, but when she repeated herself he stayed just as puzzled. "Why is going to New York odd? That's what she does. So she got a big, surprise offer. Could have been last minute. She could have been substituting for a sick model. Maybe for once she decided not to worry about homework. Left too quickly to get assignments anyway. Why would you doubt her own father?"

"You talk like a cop."

He pulled his wallet from his back pocket and flipped it open to his detective shield.

Sara didn't laugh. Instead she grabbed his wrist and tugged. "Get me more information on the car."

Not finished dinner.

I need a cop. I'll go get one. She stood up.

Steve pushed her back into her chair and raised his finger. *Okay. Wait.* He called over his shoulder. When Lieutenant Marino reappeared at the door, he turned to talk with her. *Eat. Information is on the way,* he signed to Sara as the officer left.

They had nearly finished by the time Marino returned. Sara strained to read the lieutenant's lips as Steve asked her to speak slowly.

"Standard tow. Late model import. Sedan, K-I-M-Z on the plate. The Mahoney Garage hauled it from Front Street about five-thirty this morning." She shrugged. "Not much else."

Steve knit his eyebrows. "Front Street at five in the morning? I had no idea."

Sara pressed a fist to her stomach. Front Street was the warehouse district. There was no reason Kim would drive in a place like that. Steve was as lousy at hiding any emotion as she was, and concern darkened his features. She was relieved that he was taking the report seriously, but the knot in her stomach stayed hard as he shook his head.

She looked back at the lieutenant. "I was at her house. No car returned there."

"Winchester Commons has closed garages," Steve replied.

"Her parents use the garage. Kim uses the parking shed. Remember? I almost got hit getting her car last week. I told you."

Lieutenant Marino nodded toward the remains of their dinner. "I'm due at headquarters. Steve, why don't you two finish eating, then give Vehicle Storage a call. See what else you can find out. The paperwork's been filed."

As the officer left, Sara nibbled, but the bread stayed dry on her tongue. After one more bite she grabbed her soda and paced with Tuck at her heels. A dozen questions crowded her head. "Front Street! You would lock me in the apartment if I went near that part of the city. Five-thirty in the morning? Something is wrong!"

Okay. Okay. Don't wear a path in the carpet. I'll see what I can find out. Then go home. Promise. Steve tapped his watch. Sara wrinkled her nose.

Ten minutes later she was slouched at Steve's desk mulling over answers that raised more questions. After numerous phone calls, Steve told her that Kim's car had been parked, not in a tow zone, but blocking the trucking entrance of a warehouse. The manager of a lumber company discovered it when he went onto the loading dock to wait for a dawn delivery. The manager called the police and had the car towed.

Steve explained that the automobile had not been reported as a stolen car. Consequently it remained at the police department's tow lot until the officer in charge worked his way through more pressing problems. Some time during late morning the license plate was run through the Registry of Motor Vehicles. Roth and Hubbard Securities was listed as the owner.

"Not Kim?"

Steve waved off her question. "That only means her father's company is the technical owner. Tax break. The police contacted the company at their headquarters in the Mutual Finance Building downtown. David Roth picked up the car sometime early in the afternoon. You should know there were small droplets of blood on the headrest — "

Oh, Steve! She grabbed Steve's arm.

Steve pushed her wrist down and shook his head. "Her father said that was from the cut on the back of her head when the awning fell. Remember? I can confirm the injury. So can you."

He wrote most of this on a sheet of paper to make sure she understood. Sara read as she paced again. On her second swing around her brother's small office, she stretched her fist and extended finger and thumb from ear to mouth. *Telephone.*

"No more calls!" He pulled out his wallet and handed her some money. *Take Tuck and go home. Pick up something for tomorrow from the deli. You have more important things to worry about than Kim. She's in New York. Her car is back with her father. It all makes sense.* He wiggled his fingers and yawned. "The airport has good security, but cars do get stolen, especially expensive, hot ones like Kim's. It makes sense that she drove it there to catch her plane. It was stolen off the lot which is why it wasn't reported stolen. No one knew it was missing." *Understand?*

I was at Kim's this afternoon. No car, remember?

He glowered at her and tapped his temple. "David Roth is a very rich man. He probably drove it right to his mechanic to have it looked over for insurance claims. Or maybe his wife is out of town and the car's in the garage. Let go of this, Sara."

Impatience kept her as edgy as her brother. She was a detective's daughter, a detective's sister. She knew about car theft rings, chop shops that stole parts and switched registrations. She knew about hot-wiring and pulling ignitions.

She ignored her brother's frustration. *Was*

there any damage to the car? "Was the registration still in it? How about Kim's insurance papers? Radio, CD player? Cell phone? She had the works."

Steve looked as though he didn't want to admit it. *Yes. Everything was still there. No damage.*

She jabbed her finger at him. *Understand what I mean? Stolen car with no sign of break-in? Nothing stolen? Drops of blood . . . Does that make sense?* With all the sarcasm her body language could convey, she grabbed his wallet from where it lay on the desk and flipped it back open to his badge. "Detective? Cop? Where's that gut instinct Dad always said you inherited?"

"Leave Dad out of it," Steve shot back.

If Dad were here —

Sara, anybody else in this building will agree with me.

Not Dad. He would have —

Dad's not here, okay? He would have said the same thing. He taught me — Hell, what does it matter?

Tears, more of frustration than hurt, stung Sara's eyes and she blinked hard.

Steve looked exhausted and miserable. He shoved his hand through his hair as his shoulders slumped. He circled his heart and lifted a stack of files. *I'm sorry. I don't need to be reminded that I have my father's reputation to live up to. I have real police work to worry about. I have you to worry about. Go home; do your homework. I'll be home by ten. Kim's own parents aren't concerned about her. You shouldn't be, either.*

I'm her friend, Sara replied defiantly.

In reply, he held up the files and shook them at her. *I'm busy!*

Sara slapped her thigh for Tuck and grabbed her jacket. Steve let her go without another word, which hurt as much as his skepticism.

Chapter 14

By the time Sara reached the Penn Street Deli she wanted to be home as much as Steve wanted her there. She was mentally drained and needed the concentration of homework to get her mind off what had — or hadn't — happened to Kim. She sighed and dropped Tuck's leash over the parking meter for the second time that night.

"Can't stay away," the Patrones joked as she bought one of their specialty barbecued chickens she could heat up for dinner the next night — with or without her brother. This time she had to force a smile.

She tried to pay, blushed at their refusal, and wished them a good night. Her smile and all thoughts of Steve or Kim vanished, however, as she reached the sidewalk. Tuck was gone.

Her fingers tightened on her grocery bag. As her heart lurched she glanced left, then right. Tuck! Left, then right. She hurried around people, through the thinning sidewalk traffic. She squinted ahead, then behind her. There was no sign of her retriever.

Sara jogged to the next intersection, as far as the Buckeye Bakery, and stopped at the traffic light. There were alleys between the buildings and a grid of commercial blocks. Although her first impulse was to run up and down all of them, dusk had dropped to night. It was too dark. It wouldn't solve anything. She couldn't hear Tuck's bark, couldn't whistle or call for him and hear a response. She shoved the bag under her arm and clapped her hands in their signal, but she had no way of knowing how loud the traffic was.

She turned back to the delicatessen and continued past it to the corner laundry, the direction she'd come from Thurston Court. No Tuck. Sara fought rising panic as she returned to the parking meter where she'd left him.

He wasn't just any golden retriever. Tuck was trained to obey, to wait. She'd never know him to wander off, even in a park full of other dogs. Besides, as always, she'd dropped the loop of his leash over the meter.

Chills raised the hair on her arms as she looked at the stark metal pole. Unless the solid leather loop had broken, Tuck had to have been led off by someone who deliberately took him.

When she was sure her dog wasn't going to materialize out of the night air, she started to return to the police station. Steve.

Don't panic. Don't jump to conclusions again tonight. She could imagine his fingers flying as he lectured. He'd hold up his files again to show how busy he was. He'd glower, and rake his hair. Nevertheless, there was a chance patrol officers would drive her around in a squad car — at least search the alleys with her. Surely officers would search for a missing hearing-ear retriever, or maybe the Patrones would help. Anytime, they'd told her, for anything.

She jogged in and out of pedestrians for half a block, then returned to where she'd left him. She stopped and leaned against the soda machine in front of the deli. Stop acting frantic, she told herself. Tuck will be found. He wore a collar and tags. She signed it: *Tuck will be found.* Her fingers were cold.

As she took a deep breath, a figure stepped from one of the alleys near the corner. He glanced at her, then slapped his thigh. Like some amateur magic act, Tuck appeared from the alley and trotted toward her, still on his leash. Tuck! Relief washed through her, head to stomach to feet.

Sara knelt and put her arms out, but even as she buried her face in his fur, she admonished him with a shake of his collar. When she stood up, the man offered her the leash.

Sara's heart jolted as she recognized him — Mr. No Pinky. "You found my dog. Thank you! I can't imagine how he got loose." She watched the man carefully, to gauge his reaction to her voice.

He nodded that he understood, then slipped change into the machine and waited for a can to drop.

"Did you see anyone take his leash off the meter?"

He knit his brows and arched his shoulders.

Sara tried one more. "Where . . . did . . . you . . . find . . . him?"

This close, he looked to be in his midthirties and was well dressed in a sports jacket and jeans. He pointed toward the bakery with his left hand. "Down the block. Dragging his leash. He seemed familiar with the street. Probably following the aroma. Smells like chocolate tonight." He offered her the drink. "I'm sorry you were so frantic. Have some soda while you calm down. Do you live in the neighborhood?"

"Yes. He knows the neighborhood." She opened the can and took a few swallows. Butterflies were still flailing around inside her stomach but the soda helped. She finished it. Despite his helpfulness, she didn't want to give a stranger any more information than was necessary.

She dropped the empty can in the receptacle and read her watch. "Thank you, again."

He nodded.

Spy, foreign correspondent, terrorist? Her game flashed back at her. Tuck had been returned by the man who had watched her as she passed the laundry earlier, the one entering the deli as she left the first time. He never mentioned it.

Sara left him and headed directly for her apartment, then stopped mid-block. Her heart still raced. The back of her neck burned. He was following her. At the corner she looked back. The man was in the alcove of a bookstore and stood in the shadows with his hands in his pockets.

Sara looked at Tuck. The man had stood at the alley entrance and slapped his thigh as he'd seen her approach, as if he'd been waiting for her — over an hour from the time he'd come out of the laundry. Her dog hadn't trotted into view until he was called. Tuck hadn't found her; the man had. She fingered the entire loop of the leash. There were no breaks, no cracks in the leather, not even a worn spot. She fought chills again.

By ten o'clock Sara had managed to put a halfhearted effort into finishing her homework. The minute she closed her biology book, she sat and stared at the magazine ad of

Kim that was pinned to her bulletin board. Two minutes later she'd crossed the hall to the Fletchers' and brought Keesha back.

Weird night. Lots to tell you, she signed.

As Sara recounted Tuck's disappearance and return, Keesha fingered the loop of the leash. She looked apologetic and circled her heart. *Sorry. I'd say some wise-guy kid pulled the leash off the meter and this other guy found Tuck wandering.*

"Tuck doesn't wander. He's trained to stay and wait for me."

Keesha signed *Take Tuck. Return Tuck. With witnesses? Why? Makes no sense. Want to call Bret, see what he says?*

No way. "He's angry at me already. He'll probably tell me to file a dognapping report with Steve." *There's more. Kim's car was stolen.*

Sara added everything she knew, but Keesha didn't look any more convinced. "I know you're mad at me, but I agree with Steve. . . . If Mr. Roth thinks everything's okay, it must be."

Blood!

We were with her when she cut her head.

I know, I know, Sara responded impatiently. She walked Keesha to the front door and watched as her best friend crossed the hall. No help from anyone. I'm in this alone, Sara thought as she went back to her empty apartment.

Sara rubbed her arms against the chills that wouldn't leave her. She tried watching television and paging through a fashion magazine Kim had given her. Then she crossed to the window and stared into the city streets. Seven stories below, the wind scattered leaves along the curb and knocked more from the branches of the maples that lined the street.

She was lost in thought until a figure moved next to a tree. Nothing out of the ordinary except that he had binoculars to his eyes. His head was tilted at an angle that put his line of vision at her window. Her chills turned to knots of fear.

She was about to yank the shades closed when she stopped, forced herself to remain calm, and stepped back. She pulled open the bottom drawer of the desk that had been her father's. He had his own binoculars, top of the line, powerful, a birthday present from Steve two years earlier.

She motioned Tuck to sit and with all the calm she could muster, left the room for the darkened end of the apartment. Without turning on a light, she slid back the patio door that opened onto their balcony. At this height the wind slapped at her, but she had an unrestricted view of the street clear to the corner.

She knelt in the corner of the balcony, and propped her binoculars on the rim of the railing. It kept her hands steady. She focused on the nearest streetlight and worked her way down, past the mailbox, the wire mesh trash receptacle, the fire hydrant, the maple tree. He was there, still, shoving his own high-powered glasses into the pocket of his sports jacket. She didn't need to focus on his hand to know a finger was missing.

As if he had all the time in the world, he put his hands into his pockets and walked to the corner, turned and approached the line of cars parallel parked up the street. In less than five minutes a dark sedan pulled away from the curb. As it passed under the streetlight Sara could see clearly that it was the red model that had followed her to the airport.

An hour later the blinking of her ceiling light woke her from her already fitful sleep. She opened her eyes to the familiar signal as her brother took his hand off the light switch.

Hi. He signed with an apologetic expression and crossed the room to sit across from her on the edge of her guest bed. He circled his heart. *Sorry about tonight. I was too hard on you. Before you go to sleep —*

I was asleep.

"I called David Roth. I had the perfect excuse — reminded him that I was the one who called him from the hospital about Kim and the awning accident." He tapped his chest in pantomime. "I told him I saw the police report about Kim's car. Blood on the headrest . . . wanted to make sure everything was all right."

Sara searched her brother's expression for an indication that her suspicions were correct, that something serious was going on. Instead of concern, Steve smiled and stood up.

"I mentioned the blood and he agreed it was from the awning accident. Kim's dad also said he took the car to their mechanic . . . to make sure the engine's all right. Just as I said."

"Did he say it had been stolen from the airport?"

"I didn't ask."

She sat up, about to tell Steve about the man, Tuck, the car, the trip to the airport, but thought better of it. It had to wait. Anything that would add to his concern for her or heighten his schedule would restrict her further. He'd want her in the apartment day and night. He'd put her under house arrest. Kim wouldn't stand a chance.

Instead she signed *good night* as Steve patted her shoulder. "I hope you feel better. Kim will be home in a few days and you can tell her all about the case that never was."

Chapter 15

"This has been the strangest morning." Liz Martinson arrived breathless at her locker with only minutes to spare before the start of classes. "Guess what happened to Kim's car?"

"Stolen," Keesha replied. Sara drew her right hand into a claw along her left arm to show the sign.

Steve. Last night, Sara added as Keesha explained how they'd learned.

Liz looked annoyed. "Why didn't you call me? I found out this morning. Before we were even up, some guy called my father who said he was the Roths' mechanic and could he talk to me right away about Kim's car. Before school."

Sara strained to follow the rapid English. *Talk to you?*

"Kim drove me to the Side Door Café Sunday night, remember? This guy came to the house to see if I had noticed anything — noises in the engine or anything like that, since I was the last person in the car with her."

"Is something wrong with the car?"

Liz shrugged. "I guess that's what they're paying him to find out. I said it ran fine when I was in it. I never noticed anything wrong."

"Why didn't he just call Kim in New York and ask her?"

"I asked the same thing. He said Mr. Roth doesn't want to upset Kim by having her know her car was stolen while she was away."

"But there's nothing wrong with the car and it's been found."

Liz looked hard at Sara. "There must be. He wanted to know the route we drove home. Did we go up hills — more strain on the gears. Had we been near the river — moisture. This guy might run the garage or something, but he didn't look like he spent much time under anybody's car hood. The guy that works on our cars has practically permanent stains on his hands and fingernails. This guy's hands looked like they never went near anything greasy."

Keesha laughed. "What did you do, stare at his fingers?"

Liz denied it. "It wasn't like I was staring or anything, but I noticed because one of his fingers was missing."

Sara's heart leapt. She grabbed Liz's arm then let go. *Say again.*

Liz blinked and wiggled her fingers. "Missing finger." She tapped the pinky on her left hand.

Missing finger. Sara asked Liz to describe the mechanic in detail and then explained. *Same man!* "Whoever he is ... used Tuck as an excuse to talk to me last night, and Kim's car as an excuse to talk to you this morning."

"What did he ask you about Kim?" Liz asked.

Sara had to admit that he hadn't asked anything. "He just returned Tuck. Later I saw him looking at our apartment window with binoculars. I know you both think this is a coincidence, but it doesn't feel like one."

Suzanne Andrews was Sara's interpreter, and accompanied her to classes. She sat next to her and signed each teacher's lecture and instructions which made it possible for Sara to follow every class. It also made it impossible for her to doodle, daydream, or get away with not paying attention.

Sara sat in history class and watched Mrs. Andrews' fingers. *The rich soil along the Nile is the principal natural resource of E-G-Y-P-T . . .*

Mrs. Andrews tapped Sara's open notebook, and Sara dutifully resumed taking notes. It was nearly impossible to care about the great mysteries of the Nile valley of five thousand years ago when the real mystery was unfolding right in front of her.

At the end of school Sara met Liz and Keesha at their lockers. She smiled and hoped she looked apologetic. "Tell Coach Barns I forgot . . ." She tapped her jaw.

"Dentist appointment. No crew practice."

They waved to her as she crossed the street and caught the bus downtown. As the doors closed on 61C and she paid her fare, Sara's smile disappeared. Isolation was as bad as frustration. She grimaced as she rode past Penn Square and the Radley Free Library. Bret would be arriving soon.

Kim's agent was in the Fairfax Building just past the square. That much she knew from Kim. The rest she was going to have to wing. She tried not to look at the library as she got out at the next corner and entered the office building. The Russell Agency was listed on the directory in the lobby. She took the elevator to the fourth floor.

In the agency, a receptionist sat at a mahogany desk on carpet that made Sara's footsteps springy. Glamorous pictures of models lined the walls. Kim was one of them. A couch was empty, but the phone was blinking. Sara smiled and waited until the woman at the desk was free.

When she finally asked if she could help, Sara nodded and walked to the desk. As slowly and distinctly as she could, she said,

"I know Mr. Russell is in New York with Kimberly Roth — "

The receptionist shook her head and frowned.

Sara pulled paper and pencil from her backpack. The receptionist waved it away. "Mr. Russell is in his office."

Sara stared at her mouth. "Here?"

The woman swiveled and pointed to a closed door. She pantomimed a phone and held up her hand. Wait.

Sara nodded and wrote out what she wanted to ask.

> I'm from Radley Academy. I need
> to get in touch with Kim Roth
> about school assignments. Can Mr.
> Russell give me her hotel number
> in New York?

The receptionist took the note into the office. Two minutes later she was back with a tall, fashionably dressed man behind her. He shook Sara's hand. "I'm Todd Russell, Kim's agent. I understand you need some school information?"

"Yes."

He smiled. "That's easy. Kim's not in New York; she's down with the flu. Sick. She's not on assignment. In fact, I had to postpone another shoot at Montgomery Studios when her father called yesterday."

Sara couldn't believe that she'd understood the agent's last sentences. "Flu? She's here in Radley?"

Todd Russell nodded. Sara looked from him to the receptionist. "Thank you. I'm sorry. I'll call her house tonight. I guess I misunderstood."

She left, convinced that they both thought her deafness had confused her. If it were only that simple, she thought as she walked to the bus stop.

Kim's father says Kim's in New York with her agent. Her agent says she's home with the flu. Sara's thoughts were frantic. Kim's vanished. Kim's missing. Kim's parents don't want anyone to know. I'm being followed. Liz is being questioned. What is really going on?

Chapter 16

Nothing makes sense. Sara said it, signed it, thought it a hundred times during the commute back to Thurston Court. The 61C let her off at Harrison Street and the fifteen-minute walk home did little to clear her head.

She called her brother on the TTY, and admonished him to be safe when he said he'd be out most of his shift. It felt good to turn the tables once in a while. Undercover, she thought. She couldn't ask for details. It gave her the freedom she needed.

Impulsively she yanked the magazine shot of Kim off her bulletin board and glued it to a piece of computer paper. In block letters, she printed:

MISSING
KIMBERLY ROTH
BLONDE HAIR
BLUE EYES
5 FEET 7

She then rolled up the impromptu flyer and got in her car. Ten minutes later she pulled into the Martinsons' driveway and knocked on the kitchen door. Liz was in the den doing her homework. Sara held out the flyer to Liz.

Sara apologized and told Liz about her visit to Todd Russell. "You all think I'm crazy, but I know Kim's missing. Show me where she stayed the last time."

Liz grabbed a jacket from the closet and took Sara outside to the garage. Although the apartment above it was unoccupied, it was comfortably furnished so that it could be used for houseguests. Liz pointed out the couch and easy chair, kitchenette, and bedroom. "When Kim stayed here she had nothing to worry about. Sara, if she's not really in New York, I'll bet she's got some other place like this and she's waiting for her parents to get hysterical."

"You think she ran away on purpose?"

"Makes sense," Liz replied as she looked at the picture of Kim that Sara had glued to the computer paper.

Sara tapped the photo. "The most important people in Kim's life are her agent and her parents. She's not where any of them say she is. Whatever it means, they don't want us to know and they don't want the school to know. I agree with this poster."

Sara signed as she spoke. *"I think she's been kidnapped. The way the car turned up — it was just abandoned, not stolen for anything, not parts, not the registration — blood drops . . . maybe Kim was kidnapped after she dropped you off Sunday night."*

Liz shook her head. "Not Sunday night. My Spanish notebook was at her house, so she must have taken it inside with her Sunday night. Even Monday morning on the way to school she would have had her backpack and my notebook with her. The police would have found them in her car."

"What if she dropped you off Sunday night, then went home, then went back out for something — a lipstick, shampoo?"

"Maybe. We talked for a minute in my driveway and the clock in her car said 9:09. She thanked me for going and said something like, 'Now I get to go home to another empty house till midnight when my parents fly in from San Diego. I hate Sunday nights.'" She looked sharply at Sara. "You know what, she also mentioned your brother. Something about how great-looking Steve is and wouldn't it be nice to be rescued by him . . . you know, pretend she had car trouble or something. She said she'd done it once before." She glanced at the paper where Sara had printed MISSING under the magazine photo.

Sara signed and spoke again. *"Would she run away, just to get attention from him — or from her parents?"*

Liz nodded. "I hate to say it, but you know she's done it before."

Sara left with her conviction intact, but her spirits low. Kim loved her car. She wouldn't run away by driving her car and leaving it in the warehouse district. She might run away for attention, but she'd never ditch her car.

Once Sara got home, she sat in her own sedan in the Thurston Court garage. She hardly knew Kim, but she was certain that she was right.

Digging into Kim's personality fascinated Sara, but no matter how hard she tried to come up with another explanation, nothing held water but the obvious. *How rich is her father?* she had signed to Bret as they drove home that Sunday.

He's worth millions. The reply replayed itself in her head. Sara fought a chill as she got out of the car. Someone else had to see the logic.

Chapter 17

From the time Sara opened her locker Wednesday morning, she half expected Kim to appear in the hall. She wanted to rush through the corridors and spot her outside one of their classrooms. Nothing.

After biology, Mrs. Andrews tapped her shoulder. *Sara, what is it? You're distracted in every class. Doodling in the margins. Everything all right at home?*

Yes.

Is your brother feeding you?

Yes. She smiled in spite of her worry. *Steve and I are just fine.*

You can't fool me. I'm in the business of reading expressions and body language. Your posture, your attention span — everything

*tells me something more than academics is
on your mind.*

Sara took a good long look at her interpreter and finally finger spelled: *K-I-M R-O-
T-H.* After a brief explanation, she finished
by signing, *Can you find out if the school
thinks she's missing?*

They parted as Sara went off to study hall,
but Mrs. Andrews found her in the library
twenty minutes later and summoned her to
the office. *I had no idea I'd upset anybody
with your question,* she signed to Sara as they
walked.

Mrs. Andrews sat next to her as George
Morrow, Head of School, peered over his
glasses. "There seems to be some concern on
the part of the Roths about your persistence
regarding Kimberly's absence."

Mrs. Andrews interpreted as Sara read his
lips.

"I called Miriam Roth at her office to ask if
there was more information the school
should know about. Mrs. Roth assured me
that Kimberly is on a brief modeling assignment, doing her schoolwork while she's
away, and will be back soon."

Despite her own frustration, Sara's cheeks burned with embarrassment. She apologized, replied that she was only worried about her friend, and left with Mrs. Andrews for her next class.

Bret. She thought about him all day, how much easier it would have been to have him along at Todd Russell's office to interpret. She missed him in a dozen ways. If she told him about the newest clues, surely he'd agree with her. Somebody had to.

When crew practice finished early because of wind on the river, Sara went right home. Steve was in the den talking on the phone to Marisa, ready to start dinner.

She waved him off. *I need to talk to Bret. I'll grab some subs from the deli.*

School night!

I won't be more than an hour.

What gives? As if I didn't know, Steve signed as he hung up the phone.

Finally, implying that one of her friends had visited the Russell Agency instead of her, she explained about the conflicting information from Kim's agent. "I have a question for a detective, not a big brother."

Go ahead.

"If somebody really is missing, why wouldn't the family go to the police?"

"Of course we're not talking about Kim."

"Kim or anybody."

"Okay. Two main reasons. The first is that there's extortion involved. Understand?"

Yes. Threats, ransom notes.

Right. The note usually demands huge sums of money and warns not to go to the police or the victim will be killed. Standard practice and very dangerous to comply.

"Even if you do what's asked?"

"Kidnappers are desperate people. They don't play by anybody's rules, even their own."

Sara tried hard not to let Steve see her concern. *Second reason?*

Steve looked at her carefully. *Second reason: The so-called victim is a runaway. Set it up to look like kidnapping to scare, hurt, teach a lesson . . . to somebody.*

And that's what you think. Kim might have done this whole thing herself for attention.

Steve shrugged. "It doesn't matter what I think. Nobody's filed a report. According to her family she's not missing."

Traffic was thick; cars crawled as Radley stopped work for another day. Sara swore at the streetlights and the lack of parking spaces as she inched her way close to the city square that was framed on one side by the library. She had a bag of deli submarine sandwiches, two sodas and a head full of practiced apologies for Bret. But he wasn't expecting her; if she couldn't park, he'd catch his bus and be gone before she got there.

After two futile turns around the block, she drove west and pulled into the parking lot of a pharmacy, ignoring the sign that said CUSTOMERS ONLY. She locked the car. As she zipped her jacket, she glanced across the line of cars from hers to the edge of the lot. He was back. Mr. No Pinky, as she thought of him, was at the edge of the building, barely visible.

Fear made her tighten her grasp on her bag, but she refused to give in to it. Sara forced herself to move. She walked toward the intersection. People were all around her, she reminded herself. The sidewalks were bustling; traffic was thick. Surely he would leave her alone. She broke into a run. Beads of sweat were on her forehead. Fear would do her no good at all. She had to get to Bret.

She made it to the first corner, but there was no hope of crossing the street until the light changed. She jogged in place as lines of cars shot past her, through the green, then yellow traffic signal. Red. She bolted. Under a movie theater marquee, past a bookstore, flower shop, and jeweler's. At the second light she turned around. Mr. No Pinky was there. Somewhere. She could feel him.

She crossed the street and reached the far side of the square. In all its historic splendor, the Radley Free Library faced the small park. Lights glowed from every window in the handsome Greek Revival building, a Radley landmark. A refuge. She was so close!

She increased her pace, kicking up leaves as she jogged past the park benches. Bret appeared at the wide front doors and started down the steps. She was late. She raised her arm to catch his attention, although she was still half a block away. As she did, a hand landed squarely on her shoulder.

She froze, arm in midair, and spun to the left. The Roths' mechanic — the driver of the red car — Mr. No Pinky — stepped around her and blocked her path. She tried to shake off his grasp; he held her tighter.

"We need to talk." He yanked her behind a tall hedge.

She swallowed her terror and glared. "Sorry, no dog to steal tonight. Just tell me what you really want."

"Kimberly Roth."

Sara frowned in confusion as she read his lips.

His smile was cold. "Your friend Kim has made her point. She's lucky to have such a cooperative friend, but this game is over."

"Who are you?"

The man moved closer and spoke nearly one word at a time. "I'm someone as interested in Kimberly Roth as you are. Can you read my lips or do I have to write it down?"

Sara craned her neck. Bret would be at the bus stop. She could bolt, create a scene. . . . She pretended to reach for her pad and pencil, then jumped clear of his grasp. She darted through the leaves. In less than a yard she was pulled off her feet and back behind the hedge.

"Cooperate!"

Without a choice, she tapped her mouth. "Speak clearly."

"Stand still. I don't want to hurt you. There . . . is . . . no . . . point . . . in . . . running. Understand?"

She nodded.

"Kim arranged this disappearance so she could scare her parents. And you helped her. You even pressured the school to call the Roths. Was that to add fuel to the fire? And you visited their home, pretending to be looking for Kim."

Sara shrugged that she couldn't follow.

"Never mind," he continued. "I know Sunday night you dropped Kim off at her hiding place, then drove her car down to the warehouse district to make it look as though it had been abandoned. Risky, but I figure one of your friends went with you."

Sara's breath caught in her chest. She shook her head.

He looked disgusted. "Your scheme worked, almost. The Roths are good and scared, but they aren't stupid. They're ready to file charges against you. You can forget any influence the Howell name might have in the police department. The Roth name pulls a lot more weight in this town."

"You're wrong. Crazy." Sara tapped her ears, sure she had misunderstood. "I'm deaf."

"Deaf, but bright. Don't pretend you don't understand. It's over, Miss Howell." He slid his wallet from his back pocket and flipped open his identification. "Take the card. Parker Roberts. I'm a private investigator. Tonight you take me to Kim."

Chapter 18

"I suggest you talk," he added.

She tapped her temple in confusion.

"Your fingerprints are all over the car — steering wheel, trunk. . . . We got a clear one on the door handle, too. Damn risky leaving a car that fancy in the warehouse district in the middle of the night."

"How did you identify my fingerprints? I'm not a criminal."

"Remember the soda can I offered you after your dog turned up?"

"That's why you took Tuck off the parking meter yourself, then pretended you'd found him?"

"I borrowed him long enough to give me a

clean set of fingerprints on the soda can that I could have compared with the prints the lab picked up on the car."

"The Roths had the car impounded at a crime lab? Why did you tell Liz you were the mechanic?"

"To see if she'd tell me where she drove with Kim Sunday night. To get her prints, too."

"Just playing detective," Sara said sarcastically, hoping she would confuse him.

The investigator glared, then poked the deli bag. "You were about to deliver Kim's dinner. This time I'll go along for the ride."

Thoroughly confused, Sara sighed as he finally moved her back onto the sidewalk and nudged her onto a park bench. One hundred yards ahead, Bret's bus had pulled into the traffic and was disappearing in the opposite direction.

There was no hope of reaching him, so she turned back to Roberts. "How long have you been following me?"

"Sunday night the Roths found this note. They arrived home from the airport to an empty house. They called me in on the case about midnight." He opened the billfold section of his wallet and spread a piece of paper on his knee. "Your touch, I'm sure. Amateurish. Torn from teenage fashion magazines." The note was fashioned from letters, the stuff of a hundred movies and crime novels.

IF YOU WANT TO SEE YOUR DAUGHTER AGAIN, WAIT FOR FURTHER INSTRUCTIONS. BUY THE GAZETTE AT THE COMMONS' NEWSPAPER MACHINE. WEDNESDAY 7:00 P.M. NO COPS. EVER.

She looked at the note and then at the investigator. "You were in the laundry room at the Roths' when I came by."

Roberts nodded. "If you and the rest of your friends think this is some big adventure, a good way to get the Roths to sit up and pay attention to their daughter, then you'll all be needing damn good lawyers. Last week Kim argued with her parents about a modeling assignment in Paris. They feel she's too young — whatever. There were some fights over curfews. Kim made the point that they are out of touch with her life."

Sara tapped him to indicate her confusion.

"She . . . threatened . . . to disappear. She told them some Sunday night they'd fly home to an empty house. Okay. She did it. You and Kim underestimated the Roths this time. They're not about to stroll down to the newspaper machine and wait for Kim to reappear tonight."

Sara's face mirrored her alarm. "Pay attention! I don't know anything about this note. I'm worried. I'm afraid. The Roths have to do what the note says. I didn't write it." *I did not write this note,* she added, as if her fingers could convince him.

For the first time, the investigator frowned.

Sara jumped to her feet and pulled him up with her. "Real kidnappers. Criminals. They tried before. We have to go to the Roths. You make them understand they have to go to the paper machine. Or no Kim." *No Kim! You're risking Kim's life!*

By the time Sara reached Winchester Commons, fear for her own safety had dissolved. No wonder there had been no report of kidnapping. No wonder the Roths were angry. They were dangerously following the wrong track. Maybe if the Roths had her arrested and Kim were still missing, someone would finally pay attention to what had *really* happened. Sara and the investigator had run back to their cars. By then Parker Roberts' expression had convinced her that he was beginning to doubt his own airtight theory on Kim's disappearance.

Sara parked and got out at the curb in front of the Roths' townhouse, and waited for the investigator to get out of his car. As he pulled behind her, his headlight illuminated the storm drain. Sara leaned over. Underneath a pile of bright orange leaves, the red-and-white sweater she hadn't wanted Sunday night lay tangled in the grate.

"Kim's," she said as she pulled it up. "Top of a pile of clothes. Backseat. Her car. Sunday night. Of course! She parked here to unload the car. Took clothes, Spanish notebook inside. Came out to move the car. They got her here. Jumped in her car, made her drive to the warehouse. Switched cars." *Here,* she signed angrily as the front door opened.

There wasn't time for frustration or requests as Sara fought to understand the rapid explanations Roberts gave the Roths. The three of them spoke as if she were invisible, staring at her only when Roberts pointed, obviously encouraging them to consider her explanation. When the investigator finished, Miriam Roth looked at her watch and made hurried motions toward her husband. He nodded and left for the newspaper machine at the entrance to their complex. The rest of them went into the living room.

Chapter 19

Kim's father returned later, tight-lipped, with a VCR tape in his hand. "This was inside the machine on top of what's left of this morning's papers." He pulled the cartridge from its case, and untaped a flat piece of folded paper. From where Sara stood she could see the similarity to the first ransom note. This one, too, was pasted letters.

LEAVE $500,000. WOMEN'S
ROOM, SIDE DOOR CAFE.
TEN P.M. THURSDAY
NO $$ NO KIM
PAY PHONE TONITE
4TH & WEST 8:30

Kim's father sank into the easy chair and buried his face in his hands as Kim's mother pulled the miniature poodle into her arms and began to cry. Tight lines at the edge of his mouth were the only indication on the investigator's face that the situation was far worse than he had anticipated.

Roberts shoved the tape into the VCR and after a few seconds of black and white snow on the screen, Kim burst into view. She was sitting on a folding chair with her hands on her thighs. There was a plain wall behind her. She was in the same jeans and sweater she'd worn to the café Sunday night. Sara's heart thumped painfully. She stared at her friend's mouth.

"Mom and Dad, I'm fine but you must do what they tell you. Go to the phone booth. There will be details about the money. Please cooperate. They are serious. Do not go to the police. I love you."

Seven sentences. David Roth rewound the tape and watched again. This time, Sara tracked Kim's eyes. She was either looking at someone or reading a script. Next Sara looked at Kim's lap where her hands nervously moved over each other. Sara blinked. Her pulse jumped. She pointed to Kim's father. "Rerun the tape." Kim was finger spelling! Her knuckles barely moved.

Sara grabbed the remote control and kept her finger on the play button, moving the tape nearly frame by frame. As it opened, Kim's right index finger and thumb were touching. Who would notice? She hadn't even caught the subtle change the first time. It was the letter *F.*

As Kim spoke, her fingers slowly curled together: *O.* Next she raised her index and middle fingers, and crossed them: *R.* Then her index finger went against the back of her other hand: *D.* Index finger and middle finger separated; she formed a fist and stuck her thumb through it, laid her pinky out, then spread her index finger and thumb as the tape abruptly ended. *V-A-N-1-25.*

F-O-R-D Sara finger spelled to the group with her heart racing. Kim's signing was weak and sloppy, barely discernible to anyone else. *F-O-R-D-V-A-N-1-25.* "She's sending us a message!" She glared at the investigator, then spun to Kim's parents. "Did you see her hands?"

Kim's father pushed paper and pencil at Sara from the desk. "Letters and numbers. Could have been *9-O-R-D-2-A-N-25,* too," she added. Sara wrote the numbers and letters and laid them out on the coffee table. "Could have been a license plate number or description. *Ford Van 2 5 . . .*"

"Or a nineteen-ninety model of something. Or mistakes. Kim just started practicing the alphabet. Has she even gotten to numbers?" David Roth demanded. "Ten tomorrow and now we have to interpret some wild-goose chase. What chance — "

"You worry about the money. Let me take this to Steve."

Kim's mother shook her head. "No! We can't. The first note said no police. Monday, before we thought this was Kim's doing, we lied to her agent and said she was sick. And told you she was in New York. No one was to know. . . . Then we thought you and Kim . . ." She started to cry again.

"Let me take the tape home. Not to the station. You can't trust kidnappers. Kim's been kidnapped." Sara bit back her anger. "Think about who wants to get even with you!" She got a sickening mental picture of the blonde woman in the car. Sara described what had happened at the parking shed, at the café, and then next morning at the apartment. "Side Door Café. Same place a strange woman tried to help Kim into her car. Maybe she even cut the awning. Diversion. Whoever they are, they've been tracking Kim for a week. Nearly took me by mistake."

Parker Roberts grimaced. "Possibly."

"Can you understand me? What if they thought I was Kim when I was at her car, till the headlights were blasting right on me? Same height, same hairstyle. Kim was supposed to be by herself on the way to her aerobics class. They know her schedule. And your schedule!"

The investigator turned to the screen. "I admit Kim's in trouble. But we can't let this tape get us off on some wild-goose chase. Look at it again. She doesn't even appear nervous. All I see is fidgeting. I admit Kim's moving her fingers a little, but I can't read anything except a few fists being clenched and unclenched."

You aren't deaf!

Chapter 20

Kim's in danger. Sara managed to sleep better than she thought she would, but the minute she opened her eyes, she was back to a pounding heart and steely determination. It was still barely dawn. She stayed in bed for a good ten minutes and watched the shadows cast by the streetlights, as she recalled every clue she could think of that might shed some light on Kim's disappearance.

She sat up and looked at Tuck, still curled into a golden fur ball by the door. The apartment was chilly. Winter was coming. The heat would be on in another week. She stayed in the tartan flannel pants and Head of the Ohio rowing regatta T-shirt that served as pajamas and crossed the room. Steve's door was closed. She used the bathroom and snapped off the night-light. In another twenty minutes the streetlight's buttery glow would change to the gray light of another day. Rain was predicted.

She crossed the hall to the den and closed the door, then made sure she'd pushed MUTE before she set the VCR running. Steve had already run some car checks and license numbers through the Registry of Motor Vehicles. Sara shuddered as the den filled with the eerie blue light of the television screen. It finished as Steve appeared in the doorway, half asleep and shaking his head. *I promised I'd help today. Leave it alone. Get ready for school.*

Sara realigned the scraps of paper on the desk and looked from the letters and numbers back to her brother. *Jump in, be a hero.*

Or work overtime at keeping you from doing the same thing, he signed in return.

Other school days had dragged but this was the worst. There was no way Steve would let her stay home, insisting the police would give Kim's disappearance top priority.

For everyone's safety, including her own, he gave her absolutely no details on what arrangements had been made with the Roths, or if the money would be available. All he would tell her was that Kim's parents had come up with some suspects — people disgruntled with their business practices, employees fired for serious reasons. *Leave it to us,* Steve had signed. Worst of all, she was not to say anything to anyone about what had been discovered.

Meanwhile the kidnappers' ten P.M. deadline ticked in Sara's head like a time bomb. Every time she watched Mrs. Andrews sign, she thought instead of Kim. She replayed Kim's video in her head endlessly.

Rather than wait for a ride home, Sara walked in the mist. Moisture wasn't the only thing the blanket of clouds kept in the air. Butterscotch, she thought as she sniffed the aroma wafting from Penn Street, then changed her mind. The cookie factory was baking vanilla wafers.

The minute Sara unlocked her front door, the aroma of spaghetti sauce told her Steve was home. The detective was stirring a pot at the stove.

"What did you find out?" Sara asked before she even dropped her backpack.

"That a little oil in the water keeps the spaghetti from sticking."

"Police humor."

Steve waved a spoon at her. "We ran some more checks this afternoon. Nothing comes up on Ford vans in Radley, or the county." He checked his watch. "As soon as I eat, I'm going on my shift, see what's developed. I can tell you this, the latest theory about the awning collapse is that it was part of the kidnapping. David Roth thinks he can tie in the woman you saw to one of his businesses. She might be some accountant who quit abruptly. No reason. It could be a major lead."

"Before ten?"

"Worry won't help." Steve wolfed down the pasta and salad with apologies. He nodded toward Tuck. "Get your homework done. I won't be home in time to walk him tonight. Your turn. If the rain stops and you need company, stop by the station." *Nowhere else.*

Will you be there? Or will you be part of

the undercover unit staking out the Side Door Café, she wanted to ask. Instead Sara gave him a quick hug. "Save Kim's life."

Seven P.M. It was dark by the time Sara finished her homework. Seven thirty-five. She hadn't heard from her brother. Outside the streets glistened from the intermittent rain. Leaves stuck to the sidewalk and shone under the streetlights. Even if Steve had nothing to tell her, a walk to the station and a short visit would kill her restlessness.

She pulled her crew jacket over her sweater and jeans and added comfortable sneakers to the thick athletic socks she wore. Tuck was anxious to go.

As she reached the tree outside the apartment, she pulled the rolled-up flyer from her jacket and thumb-tacked it to the trunk of the tree. MISSING. She had to press her fist to her stomach. The wind was up, but the rain had stopped. Did Kim know? Could she see the street from where she was? Sara started walking Tuck toward the commercial district.

Sara was tense, stressed by her helplessness. She watched Tuck sniff his way along

Penn Street. You're as distracted as I am, she thought. He nuzzled every hydrant and lamp-post, then raised his head as the bakery aroma diverted his attention.

B-U-T-T-E-R-S-C-O-T-C-H, she signed against her jeans as they walked. *V-A-N-I-L-L-A*. She glanced at her hand. *V-A-N-I-L-L-A*. *V-A-N*. *V-A-N-1-25*. She stopped so abruptly, Tuck jerked his leash.

Chapter 21

*T*wenty-five. The sign was nearly identical to the letter *L*. *One*. The numeral 1 was signed with an index finger. The letter *I* was signed with the pinky finger. Kim could have confused them. Every other letter had been correct. The tape had shut off abruptly. Vanil . . . vanilla.

Sara strained her memory. Sunday night at the Side Door Café. Someone had remarked that it was a vanilla night. Blood rushed to Sara's cheeks and her hands grew clammy. She began to jog down Penn Street. Maybe there was no van because Kim wasn't signing *van*. Kim had been signing *vanilla*. Was she being held captive in the block-long bakery building? Sara stared down the street. Not the bakery. She would have signed *B-A-K-E-R-Y*.

She was panting softly as she passed the deli. Not the bakery, but somewhere nearby, somewhere close enough to smell vanilla on Sunday night when they forced her to tape the ransom message. Kim signed vanilla in hopes that someone would remember that they'd commented on the aroma that night.

F-O-R-D. Although Sara knew the neighborhood by heart, as she waited at the corner for the light to change, she squinted in every direction looking for an automobile dealership. Clues. Her excitement nearly took her breath away.

Instead of continuing straight, past the bakery and eventually to the police station, Sara turned left onto Carver Street. The city block was commercial, shops on the street level, businesses above. Halfway down, a wide alley, brightly lighted by security lamps, ran parallel to Penn Street, similar to the alley Parker Roberts had appeared from with Tuck. To the right it ran behind the bakery. She could see loading docks at a few back entrances. To the left, the alley ran back to the Patrones' deli where they had their own rear entrance for deliveries and parking spaces for their cars.

The bakery side of the alley was silent. The reflected light in the pools of dirty water began to break up. Rain had started. Delivery trucks sat at loading docks. A light in the window of a second floor office came on. Another went off. As she turned to leave, she glanced at the dark street entrance on the corner of Carver and the alley. A FOR RENT sign was stuck in the window, under faded gold leaf lettering. FORD INSURANCE CO.

F-O-R-D. Not a car, or a dealership, but an office. Close to the smell of vanilla. It all fell horribly into place. Kim! She was being held two blocks from the police station . . . the last place anyone would suspect.

Fear and urgency jolted Sara into action. If she could just look into the darkened office, or get a close look at the trucks and vans in the alley. . . . As always she worried about the sound she might — or might not — be making. She had to make sure, then she had to get help.

*   *   *

Tuck had to be put where he wouldn't bark or knock into anything while she checked. She picked the spot she'd always used: the parking meter in front of the deli. *No investigator's going to take you off the pole tonight! Stay,* she added. *I'll be right back. There're dog biscuits at the police station.* Tuck gazed at her with his curious, trusting, brown-eyed stare, then sat at the curb as he'd done countless times. She checked her watch: 8:17.

Sara forced herself to stroll nonchalantly back up Penn to Carver Street. She turned left and made an effort to be soundless. She assumed city noise would block her footsteps. Sirens, trains, car horns. She wished she could remember how they sounded. How much loud differed from soft.

Only one car passed as she turned the corner and walked the half block to the alley. Nothing had changed except that the puddles were clear again. The rain had stopped. Cracks in the old paving made her walk hazardous. The contrast of streetlights and blackness made the shadows deep. She had to watch her step. One foot at a time. Her hands were clammier than ever. She reached the corner of Carver Street and the alley.

Except for the agency name on the storefront window, the inside looked clear, dark. She glanced left, then right. She leaned into a shadow cast by the overhang above the door. She craned her neck, looked up at the fire escape, stood absolutely still waiting for something, anything to tell her she'd found what she was after.

In a room behind the darkened storefront, the light was yellow. From a lamp, she decided, rather than overhead bulbs. The angle made it impossible to see if there were any furnishings — or people, for that matter. She rubbed her neck and wished for some of Tuck's patience.

Just as she was about to move, a figure appeared in the gray office, no more than a shadowy silhouette, but it was human and it was alive. She would have liked more, but that was enough evidence to get the police moving.

Suddenly the side door down the alley opened. Sara flattened herself against the building. Two dark figures stepped into beams from the security lights. No wonder they'd seemed shadowy inside. They were in black, with ski masks over their faces. One clearly was a woman.

Chapter 22

One figure motioned for the other to follow, hurry along to a car further down the alley. The one! Sara knew it the minute she saw it; it was the car that had almost run her over. Mistaken identity, she thought. They almost grabbed me instead of Kim.

Her pulse thumped in her ears, her throat, her chest. She had to take small breaths to keep from gasping. As she waited, the car lurched into reverse and made a sharp U-turn, then passed her on its way out to the street. Sara stayed where she was long enough to watch the glow of the brake lights disappear around the corner. Same brake lights, same lurching exit.

She ached to know what orders they had given the Roths on the phone the night before. Maybe they were going to get the money. Maybe $500,000 in cash was impossible on such short notice. Maybe they'd take it and kill Kim anyway. Anything was possible.

As quickly as she dared, she crossed the alley for one last look. There were no signs, or telltale tape on the plate glass window to indicate that the building had an alarm system, but she half wished it did. If she tripped something, the police would be here even faster.

Again, Sara glanced to either side of her, always afraid her deafness would prevent her from hearing an approach. She held her breath and stepped to the door. She turned the knob. The entrance was unlocked. Did it squeak? Did the hinges groan?

She closed it behind her. The main room of what had been the Ford Insurance Company was stripped of files, phones, and papers. An outdated calendar hung on the wall and only a desk, chairs, and a plastic plant on top of a file cabinet were bathed in the shadowy light coming from outside.

A staircase rose directly in front of her. She could see that the light was not from another room on the first floor, but upstairs, spilling from a back room onto the landing. Sara hugged the stair railing and tiptoed up.

A door at the landing opened to a sort of living room. A beat-up couch, side chair, and television set took up most of the space in the center. Tripod and camcorder sat in the corner. The lamplight had come from a lamp over a dinette. Along the Carver Street side, a kitchenette was laid out. A sink, hot plate, and compact refrigerator were lined up under the window.

A single doorway separated the living space from the kitchenette. Again, she looked left and right, then turned the knob with damp fingers that slid over the brass. She pushed it open inches at a time until the lamplight behind her formed a wedge of illumination. The room was half the size of the other with a single window that let in light on either side of the pulled-down shade. Nearly half the space was filled by a bed. Sara blinked as her eyes adjusted to the dark. A figure sat up. She felt the wall and hit a light switch.

Kim Roth, still in the clothes she'd worn Sunday night, was cowering against the wall. She had a bandanna tied around her mouth and her wrists tied firmly to the metal bedframe. Her wide-eyed look of fear disappeared instantly.

A-L-O-N-E? Sara finger spelled slowly as she mouthed the words. Even as Kim nodded, Sara ran to her and threw her arms around her. "I'll get you out of here. We'll run right to the police station. Do you know how close it is?"

Kim nodded.

"Who kidnapped you?" Sara asked the minute she'd loosened the bandanna.

Kim shrugged as the gag came off. "It's a man and a woman. She's the one who pretended to help me at the café so she could get me in their car. He broke the awning! I've never seen them, but they knew my whole routine. She was an accountant at one of Dad's offices or something. They keep saying they know Dad has the money; they know he can get cash. No excuses. They'll kill me if — " Suddenly Kim pulled back furiously. She nodded desperately.

With one knee still on the mattress, Sara spun as a blanket went over her head, plunging her in suffocating, terrifying darkness. The loss of sight on top of her deafness threw her into a black, endless cave of terror. Arms held hers as she struggled.

She flailed and wriggled as a hand pressed something over her mouth, through the fabric. Her kicking was useless; within seconds consciousness drained from her.

Sara opened her eyes, hot, disoriented, and groggy. She shook her head as she moved into a sitting position, but memory flooded her, almost sending her back on her side. She blinked. She and Kim were both tied to the iron headboard, but Kim's gag was gone. Through the open doorway she could see shadows and motion as a figure passed in and out of view. More jeans and dark sweatshirt. More ski mask. She looked desperately at Kim and mouthed, "Can you hear them?"

"Only one now. They recognized you. The woman said you were at my car that Friday night. She was the one."

Sara nodded. She'd been right, all along.

"Too dangerous here. Time to move us, they said."

"Where?"

Kim only shrugged her shoulders.

Sara tried to keep back the fear that threatened to well up from her chest and smother her. Chances of their being found here were slim, at best, but the odds dropped to minuscule if they were moved. She glanced around the room, then at the fire escape outside the window. Before she could plan anything, the woman came into the room and motioned roughly that they were to get up.

They were untied and hustled into the living room, then forced to the couch. The woman stood over them. Sara could only make out the motion of the ski mask. The woman was speaking to Kim.

Sara stared at a stain on the wall and prayed that a plan would materialize in her head. She imagined the getaway car careening down Penn Street, past the police station.

If she could just be in the front seat she could somehow yank the steering wheel and pull them crashing into a squad car, maybe even the building itself. She envisioned them crashing through the front window, to be captured, surrounded by the officers that had jumped clear of the car.

Hallucinations! She'd watched too many action movies. No kidnappers in their right minds would drive past a police station or put the victim in the passenger seat.

Their guard checked her watch repeatedly, looked at the stairs, and finally began to pace. Something was awry. It did little to raise Sara's spirits.

At last there was motion again in the stairwell. The man appeared and the woman went downstairs.

Kim's eyes were wide with fear. "Something happened at the café. No money, maybe. It's after ten. They're taking us to the river." Tears pooled on her lashes as she looked desperately at Sara.

The man waved a gun. Time to go.

Sara and Kim were yanked to their feet, gags tied around their mouths again, and they were hauled down the staircase into the empty office. Directly outside, the car had returned, but had been parked with its front facing the street. Sara scanned what she was able to see from the window. To the left were more loading docks and trucks. Directly across from them was another office entrance. She looked to the right. A slice of Carver Street showed, and beyond it the alley as it ran behind the shops she knew so well.

The woman shoved her toward the door, then yanked her back and threw her arm across Kim. With a harsh Wait! motion they were pushed against the wall. A figure was coming down the Carver Street sidewalk, across the alley. She caught sight of a dog first, leash, then owner. Tuck! She blinked. Emilio Patrone passed the alley with Tuck securely on the end of his lead.

Sara's heart soared. Of course! It must be well past closing time. The Patrones had found Tuck outside at the parking meter. It would be just like them to go looking for her.

The woman held her back. Sara didn't dare give any indication that she recognized her dog. Emilio and Tuck crossed into the alley directly outside, twenty feet, then ten, from where she and Kim were pressed against the inside office wall. Her heart ached as Tuck sniffed and nosed his way into puddles. As if they hadn't a care, Emilio led him back to the street. Rather then return to Penn, the deli owner went up his own alley toward the back entrance of his store.

Sara fought tears of frustration. Why couldn't he have found the dog half an hour earlier, enough time to alert her brother? Why didn't Emilio think to walk Tuck up to the police station? By the time he returned to the store, she and Kim would be gone. She stared at Kim and tried to read her expression. Kim had been watching as well. Tears rolled down her cheeks.

With another shove, they were hustled to the door. The man stayed in the shadows, but motioned that the street was clear. He moved into the light and stared directly at Sara until she shuddered. With rough deliberate gestures, he motioned for the woman to get them into the car. Sara needed a plan and she needed it *now*.

She looked across the alley and turned

sharply to Kim. She snapped her fingers and pointed at her, then motioned quickly across her chest to the car, as if she should get in. She prayed Kim would recognize that what appeared to be simple gestures was ASL, two phrases she'd taught her that first night at the townhouse. She repeated herself. Remember, Kim. Think!

Kim stepped forward then halted. She stared at Sara's hands.

Sara snapped her fingers again: *DOG*. She swept with pointed finger across her chest: *GO-TO-IT*.

Dog, go-to-it. Dog, get going.

Chapter 23

Kim nodded and spun. Sara collapsed against the driver's side of the car. The woman charged around the vehicle to her as Kim ran from the alley into the street. As the woman reached for her, Sara shoved with every ounce of strength she possessed and knocked her backwards into a puddle of water. There was not enough time to run. Instead she pivoted and dashed back into the office, smacking the simple lock with her fist. It wouldn't hold long, but it was a start. Diversion.

Hope filled Sara. Common sense would tell any criminal that a victim desperate to escape would head directly for the safety of the police. But Sara had sent Kim in the opposite direction, a dash to the Patrones she prayed would save her life.

The man threw open the car door and yanked the woman from the puddle. They gestured wildly at the office and the direction of the police station. Sara's few precious moments were gone. There wasn't time to plan anything else. She tore through the office and up the stairs to the tiny bedroom where she'd been captive. She closed the door behind her, jammed her palms against the window and prayed she hadn't trapped herself for good. The window gave. She raised it enough to squeeze through, and inched onto the fire escape. She didn't feel the cold or the drizzle that drifted in the wind. She closed the window, pressed back against the building and waited.

There was no sound, no clue for her ears that the desperate criminals were back in the office. She had to turn around and look, leaving her vulnerable to the street. She had no choice and she inched herself around, then peered into the dark bedroom. Light sliced the shadows, cascading in from the living room. Someone had opened the door. It was all the proof she had time for that the kidnappers were inside.

As quickly as she could, Sara worked her way down the rickety iron railing, jumped to the sidewalk, and bolted across Carver Street. Without looking back she tore into the second alley. The back door of the Penn Street Deli was ajar. As she reached it, Emilio and Rocco Patrone and Parker Roberts pulled her into the storage room.

As Sara glanced over her shoulder, the familiar flash of blue lights came down the opposite alley from Harrison Street. The narrow space in front of the side entrance to the Ford Insurance Company erupted into the chaos of the arrival of the police.

Kim rushed to her. Parker Roberts moved back in front of her so she could read his lips. "I saw Tuck at the meter again. Late. The Patrones were worried. I knew you were up to something. I called the police." He illustrated his explanation with rapid gestures that made her smile.

Sara pointed from him to her. "Following me again!"

"No idea where you were. Vanished. My suspicions about you were wrong, but you led me to Kim anyway."

Sara took a shrimp from the tray the Roths' housekeeper was passing among the guests, and dipped it into cocktail sauce. David and Miriam Roth's thank you had evolved into a catered buffet dinner.

Amazing mix of people, Bret signed as he came up to her.

Still angry?

I care about you. You take too many chances.

Sara stopped his lecture by taking another shrimp and popping it into his mouth. She kissed him the minute he swallowed. *Taking chances to save a friend. It's part of who I am. Black, white, hearing, deaf, cop, P.I. — look at the mix in this room, all because of those chances.*

Can you believe the woman, Marcia Williams, worked for Kim's father? He said

*she was only a temporary accountant, but
that's how she figured out Kim's schedule
and the Roths'. She and her boyfriend
planned this for a year. They thought it would
be easy money.*

Sara glanced at Bret's parents who were
signing with Keesha. *This is the first time other
deaf people have been in a room with me
since I came back from Edgewood. Look at
all those flying fingers. Makes me feel good.*

"How long will it be until I can figure all
that out?" Kim said as she came up to them.

Sara grinned. "You knew enough to get
yourself rescued. Steve even showed up for
part of it. What more do you need?"

Much to Sara's surprise, tears brimmed
over Kim's mascaraed lashes. "The most important sign language wasn't on that awful
video they made me make." *Thank you,
friend.* She raised her thumb, index finger,
and pinky. *I love you.*

Sara smiled. And signed, *You are brave.*
"Brave," she said.

Kim shook her head. "You're the brave
one. You figured it out and came after me."

Steve joined them. "Sara, try being a little *less* brave. Okay?"

Sara looked into her brother's eyes. "That's something I'll never promise." Then she laughed and hugged him.

"I didn't think you would," Steve said.

———●———

Sara Howell is being stalked by someone who knows her every move. No place is safe. Suddenly, every area of her life is being cruelly invaded. Who is after Sara?

Read Hear No Evil #3: A Time of Fear

Every day *Sara Howell* faces mystery, danger ... and silence.

Sara is being followed, and the stalker knows her every move...

A newspaper headline is altered to read "Deaf Rower Dies"; a single white rose is left without a note; Sara's dress for the dance is mysteriously slashed. Then someone threatens her hearing-ear dog, Tuck. Where can Sara go when the stalker gets closer day after day?

HEAR NO EVIL #3
A Time of Fear
Kate Chester

Coming soon to a bookstore near you.